Being Your Bestest Anthropologist

A guide to unlocking your neat self

The Anthropology Department

BEING YOUR BESTEST ANTHROPOLOGIST

by The Anthropology Department

* * *

Collegeville Press
Collegeville, Indiana

More praise for *Being Your Bestest Anthropologist*

"This book dramatically changed my fundamental outlook on yams and yam-based research."

-RICO @QBTIMETRAVELLER

"I truly was not expecting the most revolutionary text in modern anthropology to have been drafted on a Texas Roadhouse napkin, *Being Your Bestest Anthropologist* is just what this field needs right now."

-JACOB @DEADNDYING537

"Franz Boas is literally jumping in his grave with excitement. This book represents everything he imagined being the bestest anthropologist could and should be."

-JOSH @ALLTIME_JOSH

"It is a fact that Anthropologists are as god-like as a tenured scientist can be. This book expands on that principal, using Mesopotamian exempla and fortune cookies to illustrate why anthropology is the only art that has been deemed worthy to crash in the guest room on Mt Olympus."

-GOUDSWARD @GOUDSWARD

"Esta obra confirma lo que siempre se ha sabido: la antropología es la ciencia de ciencias y ser la mejorísima antropóloga un proceso lógico descrito en este libro que detalla el perfil y recorrido de otrxs mejorísimxs. Léanlo si alguna vez han soñado con ser como yo. De nada."

-ALE @COLOM_ALE

"Literally the best book we have ever written."

-THE ANTHROPOLOGY DEPARTMENT

@ANTHROPOLOGYDP

For Scooters, Captain, and the Reverend.
Always the bestest.

CONTENTS

FOREWARD

On the humid night of July 9th, 1858 a child was born in a hospital in Collegeville, Indiana. Some say the corn swayed ever so slightly, the livestock became agitated, and a small tremor was recorded as far as Kokomo. Historical records suggest the child had a calming demeanor and would gaze into your eyes with such cultural intensity that you might begin to question who you are, what you are doing in life, and how the cosmos came into existence. The child was too young to know much about the world. Yet, he would grow up to change the face of academia as we know it. He is about to change your universe.

A tag on the bassinet bore a single name: Franz Uri Boas.

You may have literally just trembled a bit. In fact, this is a common reaction to hearing the truth about a child that singlehandedly founded American Anthropology and by extension, the Midwest Paradigm that guides much of our contemporary powerhouse research. Your vision might be blurred and your pulse racing. You may be questioning the fundamentals of your anthropological instruction. You may have vivid hallucinations of your degree fading into black and crumbling into fine dust on your wall.

This is simply a natural reaction to learning the truth, and now we simply ask for you to reach deep inside your skull, past the frontal bone and parietals, and dig into your brain. If Franz Boas is the founder of American Anthropology, wouldn't it make sense that he was born right here in America? Why is this all-important, fact covered up by every major anthropological association? Why is it every time we make a Wikipedia correction of Franz Boas's birthplace from Minden, Westphalia to Collegeville, Indiana it gets changed back? Every great story deserves an equally greater backstory, and we, The Anthropology Department of Collegeville, Indiana, have the best backstory. One might call it the bestest backstory.

This is exactly why this book is so important to you. It connects you as an anthropological scholar to your true place of mytho-historical origins, and provides the foundational text for you to become your bestest anthropologist. As you read the following, you may actually hear Mr. Boas whispering in your ear, reading the words to you as sweet phonemes flow from his mustachioed lips. There may be two footprints in the sawdust as you tiptoe through the garage to retrieve your next bottle of Seagram's 7. Fear not. This is all normal, although as an anthropologist, you will come to recognize there is no objective or categorical thing as "normal."

INTRODUCTION

"Anthropology makes the familiar awesome and the strange breathtaking"

-THE ANTHROPOLOGY DEPARTMENT

T hink about who you are, what you are doing, and why you are not your bestest anthropologist. You may even think you are a great anthropologist right now, but let us assure you: you are not your bestest anthropologist. Close your eyes. Take a moment. Be reflexive, and consider for one minute: am I actually the *worst* anthropologist? The answer to that question is maybe. Actually, probably, yes. But it is only because you have yet to read this book before.

What we have done in writing this book is nothing short of tremendous: we have meticulously compiled 44 tips to help you emerge as your powerhouse self. How did we arrive at 44 you might ask? That number represents each year of Franz Boas's life after he metamorphosized into the founder of American Anthropology. In The Anthropology Department's 162 year history, we have spoken to numerous faculty from other departments, and one emotion tends to tie them all together: fear. They fear taking the introspective steps to question what they do and why they do it. They fear having to make changes to their location, their diet, their wardrobe, their teaching style, their technology, their currency, and their vehicular transport. All of these aspects of your life will change if you are just willing to let go of fear and follow our simple plan. Remember: the "The" in The Anthropology Department is always capitalized for a reason. Although this book is geared toward faculty and students with advanced degrees, the average undergraduate should be able to recognize what they can aspire to be.

As a word of warning, some of the things you are about to read will challenge you. You may seethe with rage as you learn bitter truths about your subdiscipline. You may feel personally and physically attacked by verbal violence. However, by the end of this book, you will be a tremendous anthropologist and may be unable to escape your newfound fame. Some of our faculty are so famous they are asked for autographs when they are in public, especially after purchasing items using a credit card at the local Pak-A-Sak. At the time this book was written, the Covid-19 pandemic was in full swing. This was actually a relief because our powerhouse faculty and students could wear masks, obscuring their recognition. In a post-pandemic world, you may have to find creative ways to obscure your face, lest you be recognized and mobbed on the street or at a prestigious regional conference.

Our world-class faculty specialize in each of the four fields, and you will be learning about them as the book progresses. The layout includes broad topics like establishing yourself, changing personal habits, developing yourself professionally, and spreading the word of anthropology. As you read, think about how your status is slowly changing using the three stages of a rite of passage: separation, transition, and reincorporation. Although you will not be physically separated from your family, home, or office, allow your anthropological spirit to become separated from your corporeal self. There, you can let go of fear and sponge up our sacred knowledge in your liminal state. Myth and reality will become fused into one, and cultural inversions will challenge the essence of your very existence. Finally, you will be reincorporated into your fully changed status, but you may find yourself subject to jealous losers and haters in your department. This is perfectly normal. Buckle up. Be sure to cool off with a Seagram's 7 at the end. You are going to need it.

SECTION ONE: SETTING THE STAGE

"The purpose of anthropology is to make the world safe for human amazingness"

-THE ANTHROPOLOGY DEPARTMENT

Too many academics forget to scaffold themselves with the best infrastructure available. No, we are not talking about the time that Dr. Peters thought it would be neat to stack two chairs on top of one another to deliver a lecture to students. That fall and subsequent neckbrace nearly cost us our entire endowment. We still get dirty looks from OSHA whenever we see them around town.

Instead, the tips in this section will center you geographically to allow for the best professional development possible. It represents the intersection between spatiality, proxemics, durable dispositions, and knowledge. Remember that anthropology book *Wisdom Sits in Places*? We do. We forgot what it was about, but judging from the title it likely had something to do with wisdom being attached to places. Let us find a way to attach your bestest anthropological self to a place.

1. Geography Matters

We cannot overemphasize how important your state is to your identity both as a person and a scholar. We realize that states are just arbitrary constructs, but they mean so much to anthropologists that it is not uncommon to get into a dustup—or even a shoving match—with a rival colleague about which state is more conducive to anthropological study. As a recommendation, we find that the Midwest Paradigm tends to function the best in the general Midwestern region of the country where it was developed. It only makes sense that the region where Franz Boas was born would harness his ancestral energy each time the corn grows, or when the wind drifts softly across freshly graded papers. Some call them flyover states, but we find that offensive. In fact, each time an airplane flies over Collegeville, our faculty look to the sky and silently recite a line from *Race, Language and Culture* in hopes of reaching those passengers. If you just look down, you might see Dr. Chubb deep in psychic meditation.

Indeed, the best states to conduct anthropology are not located in any coastal area as they tend to be a bit too educated and pretentious for our liking. Paradoxically, the redder the state the better. How can you expect to totally blow people's minds with anthropology if they are already somewhat open? The single best state to do research lies somewhere in the Midwest: not as far north as Michigan and Wisconsin because it gets too cold, but not as far south as Kentucky and Missouri because it gets too hot. Illinois is a bit too blue, Iowa has too many hog farms, and Ohio puts chili on spaghetti. Gross.

Canada is out of the question. We were going to drop pamphlets over Windsor to entice people to our program, but when we found out they spoke French there the plan had to be scrapped. We lost a lot of money on that venture, but luckily the pilot accepted a small deposit and refunded the rest.

This leaves us with only one place: the great state of Indiana. Nowhere on the planet is there a place more primed for you to be the bestest anthropologist. It is a powderkeg. A supervolcano, waiting to explode anthropological knowledge all over your face. You might ask yourself, "isn't there not much to do in Indiana?" Well the answer is yes, and that is precisely why you can devote your lifetime to your research and spreading the joys of anthropology. It is not uncommon for incoming junior faculty to pick out a cemetery plot after landing a job in Indiana. Think about that for a minute. Literally shaking as we wrote that.

2. Be Cognizant of your Proximity to a Texas Roadhouse

Bob Evans are a dime a dozen, and we have it on good authority that no one has ever eaten there except for close family members of the owners. Thus, you will have to make sure that the place you choose to be an anthropologist is close enough to a Texas Roadhouse—the anthropological eatery of choice. Did you know that more anthropological ideas have come out of conversations at a Texas Roadhouse than any other location *in the world*?

We are not really sure why, but maybe it has to do with the fact that there are not any restaurants in Collegeville. You might ask, "aren't you violating your own rule because there is no Texas Roadhouse in Collegeville?" Well, the answer is that having a Texas Roadhouse 43.5 miles away in Lafayette makes it extra special when we crank up the LeSabre and commute there on a daily basis.

All the best wisdom comes out of Texas Roadhouse and the reasons are inexplicable. It is not uncommon for our faculty to sit down in the private room and have rousing debates about post-structuralism, political hegemony, functional morphology. Maybe it is when Jenny or Phil gently hold a roll in front of your mouth until you take a bite. Maybe it is when we mop the floor during Texas Roadhouse trivia nights. As our students would say, those n00bz get pwnd. Maybe it is the massive amounts of Seagram's 7 consumed by our faculty. There is something there, and it is special.

More often than not, our faculty have experienced waking up in a Texas Roadhouse. Now, it is not what you think. They just experience so much ecstasy throughout their meals that they blackout in a frenzy. That reminds us of one time in the summer of 1997 where faculty were in a fantastic mood. The Seagram's 7 was flowing, and Dr. Peters was ripping lines of CBD oil from the tabletop. We were getting dirty looks from fellow diners and the waitstaff until police showed up. We initially thought they were police, but their very tight shorts tipped us off that they were likely off-duty strippers looking to blow off some steam. They began dancing on the tabletops. At one point in the evening, one of the servers put Sandstorm on over the intercom. Everything just faded to black after that, and we woke up the next morning in the Texas Roadhouse. Another time, we were driving through Ohio after a conference and Dr. Peters fell asleep at the wheel during the 11.5 hour drive. We crashed through a barrier and landed in a Texas Roadhouse parking lot. Miraculously no one was injured but Dr. Peters was never allowed to drive after dark after that. The lesson here is that if you have never woken up in a Texas Roadhouse, you are not doing anthropology right.

3. Pick the Field Site Closest to You

Let's face it: powerhouse anthropologists do not like to travel very much because it inconveniences them, and it means they would likely have to apply for external funding. Who in their right mind would take the time, effort, and energy to apply for an external grant when you have the world of anthropology right at your fingertips? Why bother dealing with obscure out-of-state laws or foreign governments when you can do virtually the *same thing* without even leaving your office? Many people think that anthropologists must travel great distances to find the "exotic." Well, they are misinformed elitist chuckleheads.

Here are some discipline-specific suggestions to make sure your field site or data are well within reach:

Bioanthropologists
If you are a bioarchaeologist or a forensic anthropologist, find some loophole to get bones or teeth shipped to you so you can store them indefinitely in a campus lab somewhere. They can be from anywhere, like maybe Europe or Asia, but you can just make up research questions in an *ad-hoc* manner. It does not really matter if it is morally unethical: you can *act morally superior* by claiming that the bones are simply "under study" and will soon to be given back. Of course, you never have to give them back be-

cause there are always new minutiae to study. Already measured a particular osteometric point eighteen times over? Just move on to the next osteometric point. That should take another year. There are 19 craniometric points alone, so that could last you another 19 years! You're welcome.

If you are a primatologist, just make your field location at the local zoo. It does not have to even be a good zoo either. We are talking like a Tiger King-style-zoo that maybe has a pygmy marmoset or two. The good thing about these zoos is they always have a fried food smell that masks the ever-present smell of animal feces. As you frame your research, *act morally superior* to peers by claiming your study is done for the sake of animal welfare. You're welcome.

Cultural Anthropologists

If you are a real cultural anthropologist, you probably find ways to avoid talking to people anyway. In reality, the reason you got into the subdiscipline was to try to stamp out the perception that you actually do not like people very much. The solution? Find a way to study passive media and call it something like Media Anthropology. You can always turn off a movie, but you cannot turn off a person. *Act morally superior* among your peers by suggesting you do not like the idea of a researcher-informant dichotomy, which is just an extension of colonialism anyway.

If you absolutely must go out in public, do not stress much about the decision: just do something you were going to do anyway and call it research. Do you like mountain biking? Study the "culture" of your local mountain biking club. Do you like dogs? Study human-animal interaction at your local dog park. Do you like food and beaches? Study the local foodways at the Indiana Dunes. That is where we have had a long-term project...*for 37 years!* You're welcome.

Linguistic Anthropologists

At this point in your career, you are probably questioning your life decisions, and that is a perfectly natural position to have. After all, you did just engage in a lengthy debate about some obscure phoneme you listened to on a reel-to-reel player in a soundproof booth for 234 hours on a loop. That would be enough to drive even the most hardened into the den of psycholinguistic insanity.

But fear not. In this era of the internets, the language comes to you. Make your study something based on the interwebs and you will never have to even leave your office. Maybe you could study the linguistic patterns of chain emails, or the language of memes, or the language of how people speak to cats on the Tic-Tac. Just make up a research question *post hoc* for a theme you enjoy. If anyone questions the ethics of your study *act morally superior* by claiming that people posting online never really knew they were being studied anyway. You're welcome.

Archaeologists

If you are a fully-grown archaeologist, you are probably reaching that stage in life where you are just a little too creepy to be hanging out with the students. And that is OK. We all get it. Ear hair and halitosis happen, and there is not much you can do about it. Besides, we know you were not getting that grant anyway because we were on the panel that reviewed it.

The key to being a powerhouse Midwest archaeologist is to maximize the amount of volunteer labor you get for digs. Scratch that. What is even more powerhouse is to have a group of students *pay you* to excavate something you will never publish on anyway. Then *act morally superior* among your peers by claiming you were doing it all for their education when really you were doing it for a promotion. You're welcome.

To find your ideal field site, take out a map. Now, take out a nickel. Place the nickel over your current city and use it to draw a circle. That circle is now your ideal radius where you can conduct excavations. You do not really need a research question to drive your excavations because what matters is that you can dig during the day and return home at night—cooling off with a tall Seagram's 7 in the air conditioning. You can work at that site continuously for 35 years and no one will ever question you.

If you are a Mayanist, Andeanist, or god forbid an Old World archaeologist, an even better idea is to not waste time doing any digging at all. Find an assemblage of artifacts that was excavated in the 1930s and was subsequently forgotten in the basement of a U.S. institution. Have it shipped to your archaeology lab and slowly find ways to analyze it for possibly three decades. Of course, the collection will not have any contextual information and exists in an ethically murky gray area. It will mask the fact that you have not really been doing any excavation. You can *act morally superior* among your peers by saying you were doing a favor for those governments anyway. You can even take the collection home if you like because it is not like anyone will notice it is gone. You're welcome.

4. Choose the Best Department Vehicle for the Price

Choosing a vehicle for your department can be the most difficult discussion any faculty meeting must endure. The reality is if you purchase something too utilitarian like a truck, no one will want to drive it to prestigious regional conferences. Plus, members of other departments will constantly nag you to help them move things. We learned this the hard way with the Mortuary Science folks. Let us never speak of that incident ever again.

There is only one vehicle on this planet that is well-suited to all the subdisciplines of anthropology and that is the 2001 Buick LeSabre. The reasons for this are clear. Its rounded contours have a soothing effect as anthropologists are often enraged by sharp angles that promote visual violence. The interior is spacious enough to fit at least eight faculty members comfortably, nine if someone wants to go butts to nuts. The car's handling is really where it excels. When you drive a 2001 Buick LeSabre it feels like you are flying through time and space. The road literally disappears, and it makes you feel as if you could drive it into the sun in one last epic demonstration of how anthropology is the shining light of academia.

The LeSabre has considerable advantages when you drive

to prestigious regional conferences. Not trying to brag, but ours gets over 16 MPG and still smells like a new car despite having transported numerous Texas Roadhouse leftovers in the glove compartment. It can go very fast as well. One time in northern Alabama we were pulled over for going 28 miles over the speed limit. We calmly told the police officer that speed limits are simply a social construction, and that our cultural conceptualization of them was different than his yet equally valid. The traffic officer paused for a second, staring distantly in his black aviators at the exact point where the road meets the horizon. His hand started to visibly tremble. We were let go with a warning. Later, we were informed the officer ended up turning in his badge that afternoon as the officer faced his existential crisis. He apparently kept muttering "speed limits are just social schema" over and over again. This is just one example of how powerful our discipline can be.

The stock stereo in the LeSabre is also a real banger. Heads turn when we roll into conferences blasting Wreckx-n-Effect from the tape deck. Sometimes Dr. Chubb likes to rock back and forth in the car so it looks like we have hydraulics installed. The suspension is just loose enough to allow this, and we have fooled many a passerby into thinking we were hitting the switches. In sum, make sure you argue for a 2001 LeSabre at your next faculty meeting. You will not be disappointed.

5. Pay Attention to Spatial Proxemics on Your Campus

Ideally, your school should only have one building, and that is the building that houses The Anthropology Department. All other buildings are a waste of money and destroy budgets. This is how we manage to pay our tenured faculty well above that national average, placing them between $34K-$37K annually. If there absolutely must be another building on campus like an administrative building, make sure to consult your archaeologist to create a campus cosmogram. They will be good at doing this because no matter what the layout of a site, it can always be connected to some cosmological phenomena if you just interpret it hard enough.

Mayanists, Andeanists, and Southeastern archaeologists are especially good at this. Our Andeanist once identified an astrological hierophany of our building orientation of 120° 47'E-298° 45'W as related to the transverse axis elongation of the moon. That was simply based on the fact that the sun was shining into a window, illuminating Dr. Chubb's collection of porcelain cat figurines.

The interior design of your office should pay close attention to proxemics and spatial aesthetic. For example, when students enter our main office, they turn a corner and immediately come face-to-face with Lucy. This often shocks students with awe because they have never seen Lucy, and do not expect to see our office assistant in front of them at her standing desk (Lucy has a bad back so we created a standing desk with several cinder blocks). The fact that Lucy is standing creates a bit of a dominance hierarchy, letting the students know who is in charge. Our primatologist taught us this.

The main office is circular and is intentionally designed to mimic a womb. After all, we are literally giving birth to our students, and this is the main place of their conception and development. After students graduate, we have them file out of the office in a single line in a ceremony representing their birth and gift to the world. Last year we had a record graduating class of two students and it was breathtaking. Our labor was well-worth it and we gave high fives to each other. We also have some thought-provoking artwork on the walls including:

-a kitty poster that says "Hang in there! Don't major in Psychology!"

-a stunning 1987 rendition of the Indiana Dunes

-a framed program from the 1991 Greater Midwest Meetings on Indiana Dental Anthropology where we brought a rival department to tears

-a framed menu from our first Texas Roadhouse event

Such artwork attracts students to the major via the kitty poster (they follow the suggestion), then their eyes are drawn to the Indiana Dunes, where culture, landscape, and foodways collide in beautiful creolization. Students pine for the idea that they too could conduct ethnographic fieldwork there someday just as Franz Boas did in his youth. The program from the meeting inspires students to one day crush someone so hard at a conference that there is simply no recovery in sight. Many times, someone will walk away from their career if done correctly. This is what happened in 1991, and is explained below in the tip *How to Win At Prestigious Regional Conferences*. Finally, the Texas Roadhouse menu lifts students' spirits by showing that one day, they could have a chair at the table with faculty, sitting not as a student, but as a colleague. Literally shaking as we wrote that.

The actual offices of our powerhouse faculty have a slightly different layout. Let's face it, some faculty get along with one another and some do not. A chair can never really plan who will be best buddies and who will be at each other's throats because it changes on a weekly, if not daily basis. Thus, the best solution is to place each faculty member in a corner office, even if that means they will be on the other side of the building. But doesn't that mean you can only put four faculty on one floor? The answer to that question is yes, so we simply place them on separate floors. It is a bit of an inconvenience to go down four flights of stairs to talk to someone, but the payout is worth it. There is one exception to this pattern, and it is that cultural anthropologists actually prefer dark, windowless environments so they can write their CBD-addled musings on the horrors of humankind. Please be mindful of this characteristic when you take campus proxemics into account.

6. Produce a Well-Crafted Campus Flyover

These days, students and parents are requiring more snap, more crackle, and more pop when they make the difficult decision of which department to attend. There are a lot of choices out there, and to compete with rival departments you really need to pay attention to how your campus is perceived.

Thus, you should take the time and energy to create a campus flyover. You may be asking yourself, won't it be really expensive to hire a helicopter or local cropduster to fly over campus? Yes, it is exceedingly expensive to do this. Thus, we at The Anthropology Department have devised a foolproof method to do something similar without paying top dollar. You will simply need a camcorder, a grappling hook, a long steel cable, duct tape, two unused film reels, and a VHS tape.

First, break out a window on the first story of a building, preferably a building that does not house your department. Next, take the two unused film reels and duct tape them to the top of the camcorder so they are set vertically in line with one another. Take the zip line and tie it to the grappling hook. Heave the grappling hook to the top of the tallest building. This may take several attempts as anthropologists tend to have weak upper body strength.

Using the zipline, carefully scale the building to reach the roof. Most roof access doors are locked anyway due to "danger" or some other asinine OSHA regulation. Now, have a colleague crawl through the broken window and attach the zipline to a chair, pipe, or sprinkler head. You can now untie the grappling hook, thread the zipline through the film reels, put the tape in, and turn the camcorder on.

When you are ready, press record, but remember to turn off the date unless you want the date in the flyover. At the time of writing this, our camcorder did not allow the date to go beyond 1999 due to the Y2K bug, so we just left it that way. Gently push the camcorder on the zipline and gravity will naturally take it across your beautiful campus, recording a remarkable view as it completes its journey. When you are finished, call campus security and tell them there has been a break-in at a window in the psychology department.

Adding music to your flyover will require dubbing, but one song we particularly enjoy is the soundtrack from the first minute of Beauty and the Beast. It brings a tear to our eye every time, and it will make you sob uncontrollably as you appreciate how beautiful your campus really is.

SECTION TWO: CHANGING YOUR PERSONAL HABITS

"Anthropology demands the open-mindedness in which one must look, listen, and literally tremble"

-THE ANTHROPOLOGY DEPARTMENT

D o you ever just look at someone and think: do you even anthropology? The difference between someone who is an anthropologist and someone who is not cannot be overstated. In fact, some of you may have noticed that it is particularly easy to pick an anthropologist out of a crowd by their dispositions alone. To be your bestest anthropologist, you need a true makeover of epic proportions that is sensitive to your subdiscipline. This section provides your makeover that includes changes in diet, apparel, finance, and etiquette.

7. The Yam Cram

Everyone knows there is an intimate association between yams and anthropology. We are not talking about sweet potatoes here, folks. They are categorically different. We once hip-checked a food caterer into a trashcan for bringing sweet potatoes instead of yams to one of our campus events. Never, ever get in between an anthropologist and their yams or you may pay the ultimate price.

We are talking about real yams. Yams that feed millions of people throughout Oceania, Asia, Africa, South America, and

Indiana. Yams that have made appearances in nearly every single anthropological film known to academia. Yams that appear in every textbook and ethnography. Yams that have launched anthropological careers from obscure to legendary. Recent postmodern approaches have even created ethnographies *from the perspective of a yam*. We have petitioned the American Anthropological Association to change its logo to a yam and to create a giant yam mascot that walks around conferences. We suggested the mascot be called "Yammy." We have yet to receive a response.

To put it plainly, yams make the world go round. If you do not like yams, you are ethnocentric and possibly even racist. You should reconsider your life and question why you were even born to begin with. If we had a time machine, we would literally go back in time and stop your parents from having sex by showing them a picture of Tucker Carlson. If you are an anthropologist, you should put down this book immediately and resign from the discipline in shame.

Now that this is clear, we can begin to think of ways to incorporate more yams into your life. We call this the Yam Cram. To be your bestest anthropologist, you must become one with the yam, and this begins with consumption. No one can live off of yams alone. In fact, scientific studies reveal the low nutritional content of yams, and suggest they do not supply essential amino acids. However, science is only one way of knowing, and our cultural understandings can convince you that yams are the single most essential food known to humans.

Our faculty have come up with numerous ways to get yams inside of you. One recommendation from Dr. Chubb is to go on a 48-hour Yam Cram consisting of nothing but blended yams and water. Such experiences can bring you closer to Franz Boas and it is not uncommon to have vivid hallucinations of a shirtless Franz Boas standing at the foot of your bed. Some might say this is a nightmare, but they are wrong. Nothing is more breathtaking than a shirtless Franz Boas, and it will give you a thirst. A thirst that can only be cured with more blended yams. Some of our faculty have dried yams, crushed them up, and snorted them.

Through this method, anthropologists have reported seeing vivid visualizations of Margaret Mead, Zora Neale Hurston, or even Paul Radin. Can you imagine seeing these anthropologists in person? Difficult to fathom.

We would consider blended yams or snorting yams to be the most basic of yam consumption methods. Many anthropologists in our department have gotten creative in their Yam Cram. For example, Dr. Johnson enjoys a yam bath bomb followed by a light yam facemask and body scrub. Others like Dr. Nelch prefer to create a yam immersive environment in their homes. This includes the use of yam-based candles, yam essential oils, and even a lamp from—you guessed it—a hollowed out yam. Our point here is to be creative and emphasize the fact that your career will go nowhere unless you partake in the Yam Cram.

8. Select the Anthropological Apparel that Suits your Subdiscipline

The ways in which anthropologists dress can tell you about their discipline and how serious they are about their careers. Many less-illustrious anthropologists are unaware there are some mandatory rules for apparel. For example, did you know that Claude Levi-Strauss once invented a very famous clothing item? They became well-known in structuralist fashion circles in France. They were a pair of slacks that rode extremely high, actually covering the belly button. They were unbearably tight in the crotch area and had a blue velvet cinch for a belt tied into a bow. Some say they were as rigid as structuralism itself. He called them "Claude Squads" and made more *francs* from his clothing line than he ever did in anthropology. Many have forgotten about this key fact about Claude Levi-Strauss.

Our advice for being your bestest anthropologist beyond the days of structuralism and incorporates many of the new styles found in the 1970s, 1980s, and 1990s. Here are a few fashion tips that will help you excel.

Archaeology

Archaeologists have always had a long history with jean shorts. In fact, one of the tenants of the New Archeology was that any field project had to supply excavators with jean shorts. We are not talking about any jean shorts here either. We are talking about jean shorts that ride so high and tight your thighs will look like two Honeybaked hams glistening in the sun. A mandatory feature is that they will be hand cut with a scissors and frilled out a bit through natural use (no cheating!). They must also be stone-washed or acid-washed, and so thin in places that you can hold them up to a total station beam to see through them. If you are brave, pair your jean shorts with shirtlessness (or a tiny tube top) to harken to Franz Boas and his traditional style. If your skin tone is lighter, you will soon look so disturbingly tan that dermatologists will give you dirty looks at the Pak-A-Sak.

In more professional settings or during the brutal Indiana winters, it is mandatory that you wear some clothing item to still make it seem like you are still on a dig. When in academic buildings, it is mandatory that you still wear cargo pants just in case you need an extra pocket or two. You can even leave a line level in there to "accidentally" pull out and make a joke about it. This increases your credibility because it makes you appear rough and ready for the field even though you have not been out for years. The cargo pants should optimally be paired with field boots. You never know when the stairs outside the building might get a little slippery!

For indoor tops, make sure that flannel is literally melded to your skin, and if you must shower, it can be temporarily peeled off then reapplied. If your flannel shirt is in the wash, the only other options are a t-shirt with a picture of a trowel on it, or a t-shirt with a poorly designed image from a field school you attended 17 years ago. All the above combinations can be paired with a ponytail tie and turquoise jewelry. Some of the most attractive apparel includes turquoise jewelry in the form of a ring or turquoise on oversized earrings that stretch the ear lobe. Do not be afraid of some bold combinations either. Red and yellow can go together just fine if you remind everyone it is your ketchup and mustard ensemble.

Bioanthropology

It does not really matter if you are a bioarchaeologist, forensic anthropologist, geneticist, or a paleoanthropologist. To be your bestest biological anthropologist, it is absolutely mandatory to have a skull on literally every item of clothing or accessory you own. If your article of clothing does not have a depiction of a skull, it cannot be worn, and you must immediately relinquish your degree. Those are the rules.

If you interact with another bioanthropologist, you must comment on the skulls worn by that person. Those are the rules, and you would break a serious social norm if you fail to do so. At times this social norm can turn into written law. In June of last year, we sent in an anonymous tip to the FBI when one of our bioanthropologists failed to notice a pair of skull earrings. It was an ugly scene. Agents rushed into campus, tackled the offending bioanthropologist, and then led them away in handcuffs. Do not let this happen to you.

There are some exceptions for primatologists. A primatologist may substitute a skull for a depiction of a primate on an article of clothing, but we suggest *you include both* just to make sure your bases are covered and avoid any takedowns from the FBI. Here are some primate/skull combinations to make your wardrobe acceptable to other primatologists:

-A shirt with a macaque holding a skull, staring pensively
-A pair of socks with a chimpanzee throwing a skull at another chimpanzee
-A pair of stretch pants with a small logo of a gibbon brachiating on giant skulls
-A shirt with a silverback holding a skull with the spine still attached

Of course, these are just some of the depictions we have seen at various meetings. Feel free to get creative and create your own combinations. We are thinking maybe a cotton-topped tamarin climbing out of the mandible of a skull. Or maybe a howler monkey howling at a skull at a close distance. Note that all of these would make excellent tattoos in addition to apparel.

Cultural anthropology
Let's be honest: apparel does not really matter because you likely do not interact with anyone anyway. In fact, you probably admit to avoiding all eye contact and conversation with peers. Our cultural anthropologist replies to phatic questions like "how are you?" with "perfectly adequate," hence stifling any chance for future conversation. Cultural anthropologists are social geniuses after all.

If you absolutely must purchase something that communicates to the world that you are a cultural anthropologist, we highly recommend starting at garage sales, a local Goodwill, or the Salvation Army. The reason for this is that they tend to have a good selection of pleated jeans, stirrup pants, oversized sweatpants, baggy blouses, wide ties, turtlenecks, tunics, and heavily soiled Member's Only jackets. Remember you are not shopping out of irony. You are shopping to show you are a cultural anthropologist that has tuned out from capitalism. On this line of thought, it is perfectly acceptable to show up to classes barefoot. Make sure to place your foot up on the table to reveal to students that you do not really care about society or its rules.

Linguistic anthropology
Linguistic anthropologists can follow some of the guidelines provided for cultural anthropologists. However, clothing on the body is not as important as the outward expression on the face. After all, you do study mouths very closely and you likely end up staring at them all day. For linguistic anthropologists, tinted glasses are mandatory even if you do not require a prescription. You

definitely want to go with that "just busted out a sentence tree diagram" type of *chic*. If you have ever traveled to the southwest, turquoise jewelry is also a winner here too. The larger the better, as it expresses your deep connection with the Southwest even if you just went through the airport in Phoenix on a layover. You can extend this theme a bit further and maybe wear a brown tie-dyed shirt with Kokopelli on it. Make sure to always sport a utility belt with a tape recorder attached to it. You never know when the opportune moment to record someone's *langue* or *parole* will arise.

For footwear, the preferred style is sandals and socks. You may get more compliments if the socks are pulled up higher, so feel free to pull those bad boys up. Black socks are typically superior for linguistic anthropologists matched with brown sandals if possible. In colder weather, you will want something a bit more sensible, so New Balance sneakers should do the trick. Our linguistic anthropologist is working on scoring an exclusive deal with New Balance for both faculty and students.

9. Invest in Yamcoin Cryptocurrency

As mentioned earlier, we tend to pay our faculty well above average in the $34K-$37K range. However, anthropologists recognize that capital comes in many forms, and that modern currency does not actually capture the complexity of all social relationships. This is precisely why we have developed a cryptocurrency that encompasses the entirety of human transactions both material and immaterial. The currency of anthropologists is called *yamcoin*, and you had better invest in it now before it is too late. A failure to invest in yamcoin will likely end your career as an anthropologist as you will find yourself monetarily and morally bankrupt.

Many of you are wondering, what is a cryptocurrency? Well, the real answer to that question is: *no one really knows*. We just buy into it because it sounds cool. It has the morpheme "crypto" in it, and according to our linguistic anthropologist, that is actually from the Classic Greek word *kryptos*. Using historical linguistics, she was able to piece together that it literally translates into "something one should buy blindly without question." Interesting how we can connect modern meanings to the past like that. Thus, if you question what a cryptocurrency is, you probably should not buy it and reconsider your life.

Our anthropological currency differs from some of the less-illustrious cryptocurrencies like Bitcoin, which is based on a blockchain made from some really lame nerdy stuff. Instead, it is based on something called the *Cultural Relativism Index* or CRI. Essentially the CRI provides an omnipotent and ethereal backing to yamcoin by measuring the rate at which cultural relativism exists among humans. It also allows for substitution in kinship obligations. We call this the *invisible heart* of the market. Notice how this is a direct rebuke of Adam Smith's "invisible hand" because no one likes to be invisibly groped by the hand of some dead guy. The economic underpinnings of the CRI mean that as cultural relativism increases, the value of yamcoin increases. Thus, the main economic driver for anthropologists invested in yamcoin is to increase cultural relativism among the human populace and increase appreciation for the Midwest Paradigm, thus allowing the invisible heart to thrive. Methods for this are outlined in the last section of this book, *Section Five: Spreading the Joys of Anthropology*.

It is important to recognize that the CRI is not without risk and can be subject to fluctuations. For example, we identified an enormous and unprecedented crash in the CRI beginning at the end of 2016. We are not exactly sure why this seemed to correlate so strongly to this period, but our faculty have been working steadfastly to correct it. The good news is that it appears to be a "bowl-shaped" recovery, with a major increase in the CRI trending toward the end of 2020. We expect a full recovery in 2021 as the invisible heart guides the yamcoin market into new territory.

Now that you know what yamcoin is, we can give you some examples of how it is used. Since we pay our faculty extremely high salaries between $34K-$37K, many are upset because it places them in a higher tax bracket. This is only fair, however, and many faculty actually request a portion of their salary in yamcoin to reduce their tax liability. For example, Dr. Peters makes a cool $35K a year, but if he requests 10K in yamcoin, it brings his total salary to $25K. This still places him in the upper middle-class of most anthropologists, yet allows him the luxury of using yamcoin for kinship obligations. Through a form of capital conversion (see Bourdieu), Dr. Peters can also make purchases with other yamcoin holders. Most yamcoin holders currently cluster in the area of Collegeville because most money (USD) never really tends to come in or out of the community. Thus, it just makes more sense to use yamcoin instead. To summarize, small changes in your currency can help you aspire to be like Dr. Peters: a wealthy anthropologist in both the pocketbook and heart.

10. Use Mood-Altering Substances to Increase your Anthropological Efficacy

Let's face it: being an anthropologist can be stressful. Being your *bestest* anthropologist can mean you are so stressed you often forget to reply to emails, turn off the coffee maker in the office over the weekend, or lock the door to the bio lab. You may find a weight on your shoulders that is so strong you might think that an orangutan has you in a leglock. You may shudder at the thought of picking up a pair of calipers to complete your odontometric opus. All of this is perfectly natural of course. After all, being a powerhouse anthropologist can come at a price. So other than yams, what types of substances might help you through the day, or aid you in delivering that amazing conference paper?

The answers to this question again depend on your subdiscipline. Both cultural anthropologists and linguistic anthropologists need some of the hard stuff just to get out of bed. We are talking about some really heavy stuff here that can be really difficult to control if abused. Yes, we are talking about the big one: CBD oil purchased from the Collegeville VideoRama.

It is no secret that cultural and linguistic anthropologists thrive from the ingestion of VideoRama's brand of CBD oil. They find it helps with calming their buzzing minds and enhancing the creative process of anthropology. If you think about it, most of sociocultural research is just kind of stuff you make up anyway (this also applies to archaeological research).

Cultural anthropologists have taken CBD oil to the next level and figured out more ways to produce dizzying states of ecstasy. The tired way to consume CBD oil is through sublingual drops just before the workday starts. The wired way is through other life hacks. In the spring of 1999, Dr. Chubb modified a fluorescent light bulb she found in the office into CBD bong. She took such massive bong rips of CBD oil that she did not even know if she was alive anymore. She just stared at a Margaret Mead poster as if she reached a different plane of existence. She got several calls from String Theorists after that, and apparently influenced the refinement of nonperturbatively theory.

CBD oil has also been used successfully to increase enrollment in particular sociocultural classes. One time we had a Culture and Food course with such low enrollment we simply threw some CBD oil in the empty classroom. Suddenly the class was flooded with cultural students, and we had a record-setting enrollment of seven that year. Feel free to use this tip for classes with low enrollment.

You may be asking, what about the other subdisciplines? How do I reach my greatest anthropological self through substance-based mind-altering trances? It depends, but there is a theme that relates to both subdiscipline and specialty. The most useful application of mind-altering substances for the other disciplines comes from things that amp you up. Let us let you in on a little secret: *it is the very thing you study.*

The year was 1987 and things were looking a bit bleak at the Greater Upper Midwestern Conference on Ceramic Profile Drawing. One of our faculty members was about to take the stage to deliver a paper and was, unfortunately, feeling a little unsure and low-energy. He ducked out to the bathroom, pulled out a sherd, crushed it up, and snorted it using a rolled-up conference program. He then proceeded to give the most legendary paper in the history of ceramic studies.

People cried.

He was carried out on the shoulders of participants and a large feast was thrown at the local Texas Roadhouse in his honor. The point here is that the substance you ingest should match what you are studying in order to get the boost you need. For example, our lithicists gets through lab analysis by crushing up some chert and just going to nostriltown on it. Our studies have shown that his productivity in sorting flakes *increased by over 240%*! Similarly, our zooarchaeologist often slips away to the storage closet to pull out a small baggy of crushed animal bone and rip a line. We found the rate of her identifying unknown bones *increased by over 225%*! Feel free to be creative. At a radiocarbon conference last year, we saw that carbon was the nosecandy of choice. At the historical archaeology meetings, crushed nails made an appearance as snoot loot. We will not comment on what happened at the forensics meeting. That is currently under the jurisdiction of the FBI and we will not compromise an ongoing investigation.

This leads us to our last point that every anthropologist should be aware of regardless of their subdiscipline: beware of seal milk. It is a little-known fact that when Franz Boas was doing fieldwork in the Arctic Circle he developed a crippling addiction to seal milk. At times, he actually referred to the high viscosity lactose as his "sweet white fairy" or "silk" (a portmanteau of "seal milk").

The main reason for this is that seal milk has been shown to dramatically increase levels of cultural relativism and has subsequently been classified as a controlled substance. When Boas was conducting ethnographic research on Baffin Island in 1883, it was widely known that Inuit traders would purposely conceal seal milk from Boas because they knew of his addiction. At times he would become belligerent and be asked to leave trading posts. However, it is widely thought that his framework of cultural relativism would not have been possible without him being ripped to the tatas on seal milk half the time. It took years for him to wean himself off silk in a Collegeville treatment center, but the heart of anthropology would be forever changed through his consumption.

11. Spice Up Your Conversation Skills

If you are an anthropologist, you are probably aware that most conversations are not worth having unless they somehow revolve around anthropological topics. We really, truly, do not want to hear about your personal life, children (gross!), home repairs, travel, or pets. Instead, you should make every effort possible to inject anthropology into a conversation. This means whether you are at school, or a party, or speaking to a non-anthropologist, you should be routing each conversation toward an anthropological topic.

Here are a few examples of anthropological rerouting that powerhouse anthropologists use. Remember that you wish to limit the amount of time speaking about non-anthropological topics as soon as possible as to not waste a moment of your life.

Example 1:

Speaker 1: "Well it appears that my son Billy will be getting his very first job at the grocery store!"

Anthropologist: "Wow. Did you know that among the Nuer, boys who have not yet come of age largely have to milk cows? That is because of gendered divisions of labor where only women milk cows. Isn't that fascinating?"

Boom.

See how we went from having to talk about someone's boring and probably terrible child to talking about something intellectually stimulating? You're welcome.

Example 2:

Speaker 2: "We're debating whether to buy a new car or a

used car."

Anthropologist: "Wow. Did you know that there are socio-economic structural factors associated with caste systems that prevent people from even having that decision?"

Shazam.

Here we were able to avoid talking about that person's boring and probably terrible car choices because they are not a 2001 LeSabre. We also added an extra guilt factor into the response so that Speaker 2 probably never brings up the topic ever again. You're welcome.

Example 3:

Speaker 3: "We are debating about going to the Virgin Islands or the Bahamas over spring break."

Anthropologist: "Wow. I once lived in a mobile home for nine months when I was doing my fieldwork at the Indiana Dunes? The view was neat because you could see a bit of a dune over the industrial park."

Booyah.

See how we went from having to discuss the pros and cons of two boring and probably terrible vacation destinations to a conversation about our own fieldwork? We did not even have to rant about how destructive tourism is to locals, not to mention the carbon footprint you create when you fly there. You're welcome.

One last tip we have is to add as much anthropological jargon into every conversation when speaking to another anthropologist. The more obscure the better. The reason for this is it makes you appear superior to colleagues from less-illustrious departments or those that are not powerhouse. Consider incorporating the words autochthonous, neoliberalism, habitus, and interpenetrating accumulation into each conversation you have regardless of the topic.

12. Anthro Hard Until You Literally Tremble

If you look at all of the most famous anthropologists in history, you will notice one thing: they never stood still. To be your bestest anthropologist, you need to learn to be in constant motion. This means that you have to be reading the most illuminating, astonishing works of anthropology until you begin to shake. Many might say: "isn't that a bad thing?" or "you may need to mention that to your doctor."

False. These are the types of things loser anthropologists say who have probably never written (or even read) a devastating book review in their lives. At first, you need to learn to tremble as you anthropology. For the novice, there is a method to do this before moving on to more advanced techniques.

Here is our suggestion:

1. Pick up an anthropological classic and set it on your desk. We recommend either a Mead or a Hurston book because they were totally cool.
2. Find two gallon-sized ziplock bags and fill them with blended yams. They should weigh approximately 6 pounds each. Set the two bags on the desk spaced above your open book at an arm's length.
3. Begin reading your book. After each page you turn, you should feel the glow of anthropological information entering your heart.
4. Reach out ever so slightly, and create what we call the *powerhouse pose*. This should consist of your fists clenched, arms straightened, spaced to the length of your shoulders, hovering above the desk.
5. When the moment strikes, slowly begin to lift the yam bags simultaneously. Your arms should still be fully extended over the desk as you lift. Holding your arms steady, continue reading with the yam bags suspended. Because

your hands are full, you can only use your nose to turn the pages now as you continue to read.

6. After a few chapters, you should begin to literally quiver. This is partially a physiological response as your muscles begin to fatigue and your muscle fibers begin to exhaust themselves.

7. Now, gently set the bags down and think of what you just experienced. This will be a wonderful moment that you will never forget.

Congratulations! What you have just accomplished is nothing short of amazing. You may even want to post your achievement on social media with photo or video documentation to reveal how totally neat you are. You just took the first steps to train your mental self to associate anthropology with physical trembling.

Although the technique outlined above is a good bet for novices, experienced anthropologists will not require such short-cuts. It is not uncommon for our faculty to achieve deep trembling states without even requiring assistance from yam bags or using a powerhouse pose. A good example is Dr. Peters. Sometimes when he reads Bourdieu he quakes with such excitement we need to clear the office and put a mat down just for liability reasons. Students often stand in awe watching Dr. Peters transcend into a shimmering cosmic plane of anthropological singularity as he achieves new levels of existence. He really, really loves his Bourdieu. This could be you someday if you only practice trembling and read the best anthropology.

SECTION THREE: PROFESSIONAL DEVELOPMENT

"How do you eat a whale? That answer is simple. Remember that size is actually a social construction and finish it in a few large bites."

-THE ANTHROPOLOGY DEPARTMENT

Many of you reading this book may think you are professionally developed. The fact of the matter is you are probably underdeveloped in many areas that you are blissfully unaware of. The reality is that many faculty and advanced graduate students are so professionally anemic that their CVs are starting to take on a yellowish hue. In contrast, our CVs are so robust they even named a hominin species after them (if you are skeptical, just look up *P. robustus*).

Writing this section is a joy to us because it allows us to give you tips on things that really matter. It puts your discipline first and also puts you first as an academic both professionally and emotionally. Before we begin, go over to your bookshelf and find any self-help books you own. Remove them from the bookshelf and place them directly in the garbage can. You will not be needing them anymore.

13. All Other Disciplines are Your Mortal Enemy

We once crashed a jet ski through a Political Science Department window.

That certainly got your attention, didn't it? You might dispute this story thinking it is just a phony thing that self-help books say to further your career. The fact of the matter is: this actually happened.

The year was 1993 and things were really heating up in Collegeville regarding a new hiring line. The Political Science Department was trying to argue that they deserved a new faculty member because their classes were always full and often waitlisted. At a campus-wide meeting, they proceeded to make arguments to the dean that their discipline was able to research and appropriately characterize variation in governance, power, and behavior. Our anthropology faculty were at the meeting and began emitting audible sighs and groans with every talking point. The political scientists responded with dirty looks and perturbed bodily postures.

When the floor opened, The Anthropology Department objected to their statements. Our main argument was that the entirety of political science is *actually* under the umbrella of political anthropology and that our holistic and interdisciplinary nature of the discipline is better suited to understand political processes from a comparative perspective. We suggested that hiring another banal political scientist was a wasted line because it was not anthropology. After all, how many political scientists can trace their academic ancestry back to Franz Boas. Can you even imagine?

Things got extremely ugly when the political scientists tried to justify their discipline to the rest of the faculty. For every point they listed, we just claimed that anthropology did it—*but did it better!* We argued that many of our anthropology classes were at record enrollment with 6-8 students per class. Agitation was at an all-time high, and many were starting to get red in the face. Veins were visibly bulging on the forehead of our linguistic anthropologist. After a campus-wide vote, the political science department was granted a new line through a contentious vote we still do not accept today. Rigged for sure.

When the dust settled on the vote, we knew what had to be done. Dr. Peters leaned and gave a silent nod to Dr. Nelch who quietly left the meeting through one of the side doors. After 30 minutes, the meeting was adjourned, and faculty began to trickle back to their offices. We knew what was coming.

In the distance, we could hear what sounded like an angry horsefly interrupted by short breaks. You see, that spring Collegeville was mid-winter melt so the ditches next to the highway were filled with water. We saw a tiny pinpoint on the horizon slowly growing in size. It was Dr. Nelch literally flying on his jet ski: jean shorts gleaming in acid-washed glory, ponytail flowing in the breeze, remnants of crushed-up sherds powdering his nose. His speed was increasing as he got closer to campus and he started to really open up the throttle. As he got near the International Studies building, he screamed at the top of his lungs, "political science is just watered-down political anthropology!!!"

It felt like time was standing still. The anthropologists knew what was about to happen, and our eyes widened. His jet ski hit the embankment and launched into the air in a blur of white, aqua blue, and pink plastic. The jet nozzle, now midair, let out a deafening roar as it sprayed stunned onlookers with more water than Shamu ever dreamed of. This moment was followed by a crash so jarring and deafening many witnesses required counseling after the incident. Dr. Nelch had smashed clear through the Political Science office landing the jet ski on the main office desk. Glass and posters of Washington D.C. flew everywhere. Signed posters of Dan Quayle fell softly in the sky. Thankfully, no one was injured, and Dr. Nelch staggered away from the scene with only minor scratches and slight damage to his polarized glasses.

Afterward, the dean approached us. She said, "you know what? I changed my mind."

A small grin appeared on the faces of our faculty.

"You all were right. Political Science is just watered-down, toothless political anthropology. I am going to give you the hiring line instead."

A sudden cheer filled the air as anthropologists shouted in riotous bliss. Students ran to Dr. Nelch and high-fived him, lifting him on their shoulders. A small child in a Babylon 5 shirt gave us a thumbs up. This is how we got our hiring line for our dental anthropologist, and it was truly unforgettable.

Of course, this was only one incident, but you should be aware of this simple fact: all other disciplines are your mortal enemy because they are likely just lame versions of anthropology. Think about it for a second, if anthropology studies the entirety of human experience from our earliest ancestors to the contemporary language of lolspeak, *how is there any room for other disciplines anyway?* We all know the periodic table is just a social construction. History is just flimsy ethnohistory by people in pink polo shirts who want to talk about Nazis (gross!). Film Studies is just a pallid form of Visual Anthropology with no point. Do not even get us started on Psychology, discussed below in the section *Sigmund Freud was a Cokehead Intellectual Lightweight*. The list goes on and on. Trust yourself, trust your discipline, and if there is ever a dispute, feel free to just crash a jet ski through a rival department's window.

We did. You can too.

14. Art of the Devastating Book Review

Academic books are a dime-a-dozen: they are so easy to write that our faculty never even bother to write them anyway. Who wants to write something that can be put on a dusty shelf and used against you decades down the road? We still have faculty refuting Morgan and Tylor, and they were published 150 years ago! So ask yourself: why would anyone open themselves up to that level of scrutiny that transcends eternity? Therefore, to truly reach your full potential and be your bestest anthropologist, you must be wary of coming up with any new ideas on your own. Instead, make a name for yourself using a time-honored technique: publishing a devastating book review in a prestigious local or regional journal.

The first foundational method of constructing a devastating book review is to become mentally entrenched in the Midwest Paradigm. You might ask, well what exactly *is* the Midwest Paradigm? The Midwest Paradigm is the theoretical angle you will develop after reading this book. In a way, it evades any definition and does so deliberately to avoid scrutiny. How can you critique something that is not actually defined? This is what makes the Midwest Paradigm superior to all other anthropological theories.

Being a staunch proponent of the Midwest Paradigm means that any other theoretical perspective is simply wrong and laughable. This should be the main thrust of your devastating book review. Often this means you do not even have to read the book itself, and instead just read the cover or first few pages.

You will know the book is awful because they do not use your theoretical foundations. Is there a whiff of post-modernism? Immediately equate the book to a naval-gazing diary that you found tucked away in a local YMCA locker. Is there a whiff of Marxism? Immediately destroy the book for using 19th-century European-derived theories that are dated. Compare the book to the rantings of a poorly educated college sophomore who saw some Marx memes on an internet chat room. Is there a whiff of functionalism? Immediately liken the work with some kind of auto repair manual that an engineer wrote after huffing windshield washer fluid. Plus, Malinowski was a closet racist, and you can just throw that in there whether it applies or not just to get your point across that the book was terrible. Remember: no matter how good an author is, they are always wrong because they chose the wrong theoretical perspective to begin with.

Successful devastating book reviews will also ignore the bulk of the work and pick out the tiniest detail to crush an author's soul. Some of our best reviews have been finding a single sentence, taking it out of context, and writing 500-750 words about why that sentence was incorrect and misguided. One of our faculty members actually holds a record for writing an entire book review about a flaw they found in one of the tables. Turns out they confused a percentage with a proportion and did not catch it in the proof stage. Can you imagine doing something so unbelievably erroneous? 100% of powerhouse anthropologists would never do that.

Writing devastating book reviews should make you feel

great about yourself and bring the author of the book to tears. It is fairly common that the author will feel so inadequate they will quit the profession entirely. We once wrote a book review that was so devastating we convinced the institution that granted the author's Ph.D. to actually rescind their doctorate. Remember it is not even what you say, it is how you say it. If you use terminology that is sarcastic enough, it will persuade others that the book was really that bad. You can then post your devastating book reviews to social media in an attempt to persuade others to also not like the book. In sum, keep your friends close and treat your enemies to devastating book reviews.

15. Score Prestigious In-House Grants

As mentioned previously, external grants are a waste of time because real powerhouse anthropologists tend to not travel very far from their home institutions. Plus, competition for national grants is too difficult and time-consuming, and you simply cannot afford to lose face if your grant is rejected. Odds are that you do not really even want to do the work you outlined, and you will just pawn most of it off on some rando graduate student anyway.

Despite the lameness of external grants, you will want to apply for at least some type of grant just to keep your CV fresh and current. We recommend only applying for prestigious in-house grants from your institution to fulfill your needs, provide for your department, and achieve a campus-wide reputation for being the bestest. Such grants are easy to get if you use our time-honored techniques, and you can rake in insane amounts of funding be-tween the $250-$300 range to support a year's worth of research or tech support.

First, you will want to avoid any in-house grant that is overly competitive as you risk alienating yourself from other jeal-ous faculty if you win them. Instead, we suggest going for some tried-and-true grants that are hailed as competitive, but everyone knows you just get the money anyway. These are usually listed as Faculty Development Grants, and everyone knows that you can just put something down on paper and you will get it approved. No one in administration really has time to read them anyway and you can use this to your advantage. Our linguistic anthropologist once got a grant titled *Phonological Changes in Arnold Schwarzenegger's Accent from Conan the Barbarian to Jingle All the Way*. Really, all they wanted to do that summer was watch some Arnold movies and get paid a cool $100 for it. This was a source of great pride for our department when it was announced in a campus-wide e-mail. It also appeared on the powerpoint slides that run on the CRT monitor in the lobby of the admin building. Literally shaking just thinking about that.

Other suitable grants are prestigious in-house technology grants where you can jazz it up using a title to sound more academic. For example, titling a grant *Request for a Palm Pilot Docking Station for the Bioanthropology Lab* is painfully banal and will not catch anyone's eye when it is listed on your CV. Instead, you can title it something along the lines of *Experiential Learning through Palm Pilot Technology: An Active Pedagogical Approach for Students*. Re-read that title for a second. You would fund it without even reading it, right? So would reviewers. That is because it hits you at the core with language that speaks to the academic brain. As soon as the words "experiential," "active," and "pedagogical" are used in a grant, the outside world fades away into blackness as you envision the incredible things students will be doing with those Palm Pilots. In your dream-like state, you can see students lifting the Palm Pilots to curious eyes, even hearing the taps of the stylus on the screen as each data point enters both the device and the inquisitive mind. Believe it or not, this was a real title of a prestigious in-house grant that we got funding for last year.

We find that the use of the word "pedagogical" lifts grants from nothingness to somethingness and should be used in nearly every grant title. Dr. Peters has used the term in at least 27 in-house grants over the years and has supplied The Anthropology Department with everything from new camcorders to a new ink-jet printer in the archaeology lab. In fact, we nicknamed Dr. Peters a "pedag-phile" because he loves using "pedagogical" so much in his titles. We even got him a shirt that says "#1 PEDAG-PHILE" that he occasionally wears to departmental picnics. He sometimes gets strange looks from other people in the park, but that is likely because they are ignorant about academia and grant writing. In sum, being your bestest anthropologist means learning to hack the minds of reviewers when writing prestigious in-house grants. Start practicing today.

16. National Conferences are Boring and Pointless

Even though we sometimes attend them just to get out of teaching for a week, we actually have a strong aversion to the national conference. Step back and think about it. What is more boring and pointless than a meeting designed to bring some of the foremost minds together in some wretched city that is not even in Indiana?

We find that national conferences are really just excuses to quarrel with the academic elite, spout out 15 minutes of nonsense on a podium, and destroy hotel bathrooms while hopped up on CBD oil. They are fine to get out of town for a week, which is actually why most of our faculty attend all of the flagship conferences each year. When you add the American Anthropological Association Meetings, Society for American Archaeology Meetings, American Association of Physical Anthropology Meetings, and the Society for Linguistic Anthropology Meetings together it equals about four to five weeks that you do not have to be at school. This dramatically shortens your semester and allows you to have your TA show some cool videotapes while you are gone. It does not matter if students have already seen *Ongka's Big Moka* nine times, the tenth time is when it really sets in.

If you do not have the resources, we suggest you skip national conferences for the more prestigious elite regional conferences, preferably those with at least 8 to 10 words in the title. We have even created a handy algorithm to judge whether you should attend. We discovered that the conference impact factor (CIF) is directly related to the length of the title when comparing two conferences. For example, the Greater Northwestern Conference on Prehistoric Indiana Zooarchaeology and Identity is far more prestigious than the Society for American Archaeology Meetings when using CFI calculations. The number of words in each creates a ratio of 9:5 or an impact factor of 1.8 for the GNCPIZI, whereas the SAA only has a CIF of 0.55, which is extremely weak by comparison. When reviewing CVs for hiring, tenure, and promotion, you should remember that the conference impact factor is of utmost importance. Because of this, many of our faculty only attend prestigious conferences each year, which is the subject of our next tip.

17. Winning at Prestigious Regional Conferences

As mentioned above, national conferences are designed basically for sad, lonely academics who would never travel on their own to see a different part of the country. Since you are a happy and popular academic, we recommend attending prestigious regional conferences within a 350 mile radius of your school. The reason you will be attending, however, is not to meet people or learn anything, but to *win* the conference. You may be asking yourself, "isn't it a conference and not a competition?" Our response is to stop being so structuralist and binary with either/or statements and consider it to be *both a conference and a competition*. Here we give advice on not just attending, but actually winning at the prestigious regional conference to be your bestest anthropologist.

First, you should ask yourself a question: should you present a paper or just attend? Remember that even if you have nothing new to say, you should be presenting a paper at every prestigious regional conference even if it is literally the same paper. Just change the title slightly, or just have someone add your name to a paper you really had nothing to do with. Our Mayanist has been delivering the same paper *for 35 years* and no one has said a word because he is old and quite the firebreather. This will help to add to your CV, and also means you can rake in sweet travel funds from your institution sometimes totaling up to $25! This should pay for your gas money and hotel room when you split it with the eight other faculty members in attendance.

Titling your paper

Before even attending your conference, the first thing you should be cognizant of is the paper title you submit. Much like the title of the conference itself, your title should be significantly longer and more detailed than your peers. This will make them shudder with horror as they read through the program and realize their paper title is only a mere 12 words while your title is 33 words and almost borderlines on a paragraph in length. The longest title The Anthropology Department ever got printed in a program was a whopping 87 words, and absolutely should have been caught by the conference chair or program designer. We were told that many participants canceled at the last minute after seeing the sheer, whopping length of our title. This was actually the first step in winning: live in the head of your academic opponents and make them pay you the rent.

Aside from title length, there are some other suggestions to help your paper title be the best in show. No matter what, your paper title must contain the most outrageous pun known to humankind, followed by a colon. If it does not contain this, it should not be submitted. We are talking about a pun so groan-worthy it might actually cause someone's eyes to permanently roll back into their head so they can never see their firstborn child ever again. The pun should be so bombastic that one re-reads it in disbelief, wondering how someone could come up with it, let alone have the gall to print it for all the academic community to see. What this strategy does is reveal your confidence so that the opinion of your peers no longer matters. Also remember: word choice matters. If you are a cultural anthropologist, your title must include the words "hegemonic discourse" or "durable dispositions" otherwise you should never dream of submitting it.

Here are some of our examples from recent years from our power-house faculty and students:

-"Instant Korma's Gonna Get You: Frozen International Foods

and Hegemonic Discourse in the Northwestern Indiana World System"

-"We Are the Chimpions: The Formation of Dominance Hierarchies among *Pan troglodytes* at the Kokomo Adventure Zoo, Zipline, 'n Tan"

-"Are We There Yeti?: The Socioeconomics and Hegemonic Discourses of Truckbed Coolers at the Greater Indiana Dunes, LaPorte County, Indiana"

-"You're Fired: Investigating Interstitial Water and Volatile Loss in Amorphous Metakaolinite in Ceramics from the Collegeville Site"

-"Low Brow Humor: The Relationship Between Caudate Nucleus Formation and Joking Among Early Hominin Species"

-"I Like Big Tuts and I Cannot Lie: Report on an Extra-Large Unprovenienced Sarcophagus Found in the Storage Closet of the Jasper County Historical Society"

-"War. What is it Good For?: Negotiating Durable Dispositions among Card Players in the Greater Collegeville Region"

-"The Social Constructs of How Time Slows Down Whenever an Eagles Song is Playing"

Conference day

When you arrive at the conference, you should already be wearing the appropriate anthropological apparel for your discipline (see Tip #8). This includes: your field pants, flannel, boots, and turquoise jewelry (archaeologists); your mandatory skull on literally everything you own (bioanthropologists); the stuff you just bought from the Goodwill (sociocultural and/or linguistic anthropologists). This will help you blend in a bit with the crowd, but also show that you are serious about your discipline. We recognize that if you are a bioarchaeologist it could a bit of a challenge. After all, you are kind of a watered-down version of both an archaeologist and a bioanthropologist, so just maybe wear a flannel with a skull shirt underneath it and call it a day. You will likely look like a wreck anyway because we all know presenters really just spent the night before writing their papers. Pro tip: finish writing your paper during other presenter's presentations the day of the conference. This works particularly well if you are scheduled for the late afternoon. You probably were not going to listen to the other presenters anyway.

On the morning of conference day there will probably be some store-bought pastries and coffee served. Both will taste terrible but will calm your anxiety as you sip on coffee that is so bitter and burned you would think it was the flavor of evolutionary psychology. As you enjoy your treats, size up the room. If this is the first day of your first conference ever, find the biggest, most famous anthropologist in the room and just jack 'em. Just hip-check them into the recycling bin, the conference display poster, or whatever will turn the most heads. This is to let other participants know how you roll and will establish you as an anthropologist who cares so deeply about the discipline you are willing to do anything for it. If event security shows up, just tell them you slipped on some coffee while staring intensely with a slight grin. You know exactly what you did.

Now it is time for introductions! Make sure to mingle with your colleagues and engage in phatic conversation until you get bored and nearly pass out, requiring hospitalization. You can ask people where they work and feign interest as you slowly look down at your flip phone to see if you received any messages. Act like you have a cough and take a little nip of Seagram's 7 out of a flask. Remember: if you are a southeastern archaeologist you should never, under any circumstances, ask anyone about their research if it is not in the southeast. To do so would be to subtlety acknowledge that there is more interesting archaeology outside of your field site located just down the road. You put in a herculean effort to detect those soil changes this summer, so you cannot let it go to waste by having the conversation shift to the Andes or Mesoamerica. Remember, the goal here is to win, not to make friends.

Presentations
One way to win at a conference is to actually volunteer to be a

chair of a session. This means that you will be providing some of the technology that participants will use. If you take this route, make sure to grab one of the old laptops from the bioanthropology lab and use it as the main computer to run the presentations. The laptop will likely have Windows 98 on it, so it will be enjoyable to watch other participants puzzle over how they can get their flash drive to work on a computer with no USB drive. Shrug your shoulders and observe the chaos as participants scramble to find a computer with both a floppy drive and a USB drive to make their transfer. Better yet, suggest they try to download it from the internet and just watch that Netscape icon spin. Remember to say, "I didn't think this would happen," and "it is just my laptop."

Another benefit of the Windows 98 laptop is watching the actual PowerPoint presentations of your peers. Because the system is outdated, many animations, formatting, and images will fail to load in real-time. The images might be so large that they lock up the computer, forcing a shutdown and perhaps even a lengthy update upon reboot. This will totally throw off your academic competitors as they try to present through the bedlam. Make sure to let out small but audible sighs as they struggle to click on the laptop (spoiler: the trackpad does not even work!). Let a perverse grin wash across your face. Deep down you know you could have brought your personal laptop that runs Windows XP, but you did not.

Luckily, your presentation is prepared solely with overheads. Nothing can possibly go wrong with using overheads, so they are the media of choice for most powerhouse anthropologists. There is nothing like the smell of a fresh plastic overhead as soon as it hits the brightly lit tray. Literally shaking as we wrote that. Students really love them too for that classic analog feel. Because all the other presenters are having so much trouble, you appear as a shiny, prepared anthropologist at the podium.

Prior to going on stage, it is customary to freshen up by ripping a little nosecandy that relates to your paper topic (see Tip #10). You may be a bit nervous, but since you are about to unleash anthropology beast mode on anyone listening, and it is best to just relax and let the spirit of Franz Boas flow through you. That trembling you feel is just Franz Boas trembling alongside you in anthropological ecstasy.

One of the most basic tips for your presentation concerns time management. To establish dominance at a regional conference, always make sure to go over your allotted time limit by at least 1/2 of the suggested time. For example, if you are only given 15 minutes for a paper, make sure that it goes for 22.5 minutes. Going over your time communicates to the audience that your paper topic is so fascinating that there is literally no way you could have shortened it. Our dental anthropologist once gave a paper on inter-cusp variability for 34.5 minutes, which was a record for the Second Annual Regional Conference on Northwestern Indiana Dental Morphology and Pathology. At the end of the paper, participants were so stirred and enthralled they erupted in thunderous cheers and carried her out of the room on their shoulders.

Another strategy for delivering a powerhouse paper is to act like you are teaching the audience. Reading a paper is boring, so throw away your notes at the last minute and just freeball it. If you have a lengthy field story you want to share that is an inside joke with someone in the room, by all means, tell it! Even if 99.99% of the people in the room do not get it, you reached that 0.01% with a chuckle and that is what matters. If you choose to do this, remember to adopt a tone that is slightly patronizing to make your audience feel like uneducated students. This will also help you exceed your time limit as you really do not have anything to tether you to a structure. Remember: it is not really what you say, it is how you say it. Peers in the audience will never forget how educated they were by you. Your erudite personality will live long beyond your paper, and you will feel the feeling of sweet conference victory.

Conference badges

Picture this in your head: a white 2001 LeSabre pulls up next to you at a stoplight in Kokomo Indiana. You are there for the Central

Indiana Conference on Food and Society in Midwest Cultures. Out of the corner of your eye, you notice several individuals dressed like anthropologists flashing something at you. They are shaking their conference badges like a thick set of plasticized notecards tied around their necks. You are immediately mentally humiliated. You begin to reconsider where your career went wrong. Suddenly, the light turns green and the LeSabre opens up the throttle, leaving you at the stoplight in a state of stupor and shame. You may have just lost this conference.

There is nothing more important than a well-executed display of a conference badge. Some academics tend to clip it to their pants or dress in a non-descript location. Others tend to wear it with the assistance of a lanyard. You may be surprised however to learn that both methods are wrong in both theory and practice. Conference badges are the single most important trophy of going to a conference and you should save them at all costs. After all, part of your soul is now embedded in that badge and it should be treated as an inalienable possession. Fun fact: much of Annette Weiner's writings were influenced by The Anthropology Department's social use of conference badges.

Because conference badges are eternally connected to you, it means that *you should be wearing every conference badge you have ever acquired in your career.* The appropriate place to display them is around your neck where they can be restrung into a necklace with each badge parallel to one another. A different method is to wear them like a necklace so they stack over each other, forming a bulky mass on your chest. Some of our faculty have so many conference badges they have trouble reading their papers because they obscure their vision. If done correctly, it should look like a freaking bible up there.

The reason you should do this is for prestige. In a way, being your bestest anthropologist means not just showing what you *could be* but also *where you were.* If a peer or audience member thinks this is your first regional conference, you have already lost the battle. Your peers should gaze upon your badges with terror and trepidation as they realize they have only been to 2-3 regional conferences compared to your 113. Using badges as an outward expression of prestige is so important that our faculty often wear them around campus or to intimidate interviewees.

A secondary function of saving every conference badge is purely monetary. There is an off chance that a conference will re-cycle a logo or design and you can simply flash your old one to save on the registration fee. However, to keep your count up you must make sure to steal someone else's off the registration table. The best way to do this is to tell the volunteer that you do not see your name on any badge but you registered. As they turn around to look in some of the boxes, grab some poor sap's badge off the table. Use a sharpie to cross out their name and write yours in. You can add the badge to your collection around your neck. You're welcome.

18. Be Creative with Your CV

Did you know that the abbreviation "CV" is short for the Latin phrase *cacophonous vacuum*? It is because most CVs back in Roman times sucked really loudly. Even in this modern age, it is quite possible that your CV is a cacophonous vacuum as well. CVs are important because they are often the first line of professional rec-ognition you receive when applying to an academic position, pro-motion, in-house grant, or maybe just something part-time at the Pak-A-Sak. Thus, the structure and appearance of your CV are of utmost importance if you want to elevate yourself to being your bestest anthropologist.

There are several ways to make your CV jump out to future search committees and employers. The first method is to be very picky about font selection. The most terrible fonts to use for a CV are Times New Roman, Arial, or Calibri. Those fonts are for loser academics that have probably never written a devastating book review in their lives. We find that the best fonts grab the attention of your reader and show that you are willing to go to the next level. Of course, we are talking about using Comic Sans as the font of choice. If anyone tells you otherwise, tell them to go straight to heck. They clearly know nothing about academia or how the sausage is made. There are some who argue that Comic Sans was actually designed just for CVs and departmental posters. Here are some examples of what not to do and how to improve it:

Tired CV Header:

YOUR NAME
CURRICULUM VITAE
1/1/1996

PROFESSIONAL AFFILIATION AND CONTACT INFORMATION:

Your Name
The Anthropology Department
218 Anthropology Building #304
Collegeville, IN 47978

Wired CV Header:

YOUR NAME
CURRICULUM VITAE
1/1/1996

PROFESSIONAL AFFILIATION AND CONTACT INFORMATION:

Your Name
The Anthropology Department
218 Anthropology Building #304
Collegeville, IN 47978

As one can see, the difference is shocking and clear. The eyes are immediately drawn to the Comic Sans version of the CV. It just appears more inviting and fun, and everyone knows that you are totally neat if you just use the right font.

Another tip to strengthen your CV is to answer this simple question: who are you, both real and imagined? To be honest, the weakest CVs that come across our desk are the truthful ones. Who wants to read a two-page CV when they can read a nine-page CV that is full of personal flourishes and imagined details about an applicant's life? For example, if you were a Boy Scout or Girl Scout in High School, you should be sure to include it because it attests to your character. Maybe leave out the fact that you played the trombone because that might hurt your reputation just a bit. In fact, definitely leave that one out.

Make sure to reclassify everything that you have done professionally in a more powerhouse way on your CV. For example, if you are a recent Ph.D. on the job market or a junior scholar looking for tenure, you may want to reclassify what you consider a "grant." What is a grant anyway? It is money, right? It may be true that you did not get a grant to do your research, but that does not mean you cannot list the money your mom gave you as a grant. Maybe just call her a "Private Donor" and throw it in there. Extra line, extra fine.

In addition to reclassifying reality, if your CV is thin try to imagine what you can be and just list that too. For example, if you have zero teaching experience, just list a massive number of courses *you feel you are prepared to teach*. You could create a subheading called "Courses Taught" and just start listing every course known to anthropology. By the time a reader gets to the end, they will be convinced that you have the experience to teach everything, even though you have only taught in your dreams and maybe never even stepped foot in a classroom. Remember: each additional line on your CV is one step closer to realizing your bestest self and making your colleagues foam at the mouth with professional jealousy. Feel free to look at the next tip to assist with this recommendation.

19. Always Give (and Win) Massive Amounts of Internal Awards

Haters and jealous folks, don't read the following: our department gave out 17 paper awards to our 9 undergraduate students this year. In addition to this, we also gave out 24 awards to our 9 faculty and 2 staff members. This means one thing, and it is earth-shattering: The Anthropology Department is the most awarded department in the country. It is also probably the most awarded anthropology department *in the world*.

One might be thinking, why are there so many awards given out? Well the answer to that question is that we are just that amazing and that awards tell you that you are valued. They give you an extra spring in your step as you skip to class in your New Balance shoes. Additionally, awards provide an appropriate way to communicate with parents that your degree in anthropology means something much more: it is literally a mark of your social presence. It is true that the awards are non-monetary, but as we teach in all of our economic anthropology classes, money is just something that is just socially constructed anyway. In a sense, our awards become our social currency and cultural capital. Just think about that for a second.

We find if there is not an award for something we just make one up and add it to our annual awards ceremony. Remember to be as specific as possible. For example, you can make an award for best yam paper submitted to a particular class. Maybe you can make an award for the neatest student or faculty member. Create a random award named for a current faculty member and just have them choose a student of their liking. Remember that often times student awards are simply given out to who we like the best, meaning that we reinforce the behavior of students who act in an obsequious manner toward faculty members.

Sometimes you may have to even make your case for a particular award. Gaslight award committees into thinking they are the crazy ones for not giving you the award. If you did not receive it, create chaos. Question the results. Demand a revote. Do not concede. Blame it on the deep state that seeks to diminish Midwest Paradigms. Do everything in your power to overturn the decision even if it means looking foolish on a world stage. Peers will regard you as having passion, which is sometimes better than having facts.

Internal awards make the anthropological world go round, and if you are not giving and receiving massive amounts of them, you will be left out in the cold. Keep this in mind with our discussion of CVs above. One time we had an applicant for a faculty line who actually had no publications, but 37 internal awards listed. That person got hired while the other finalist with 37 publications did not. The reasoning for this is clear. It tells you the candidate was valued by someone, somewhere, for something. If that does not put you on top of a pile, then what would?

20. Improve your Fax Signature

This is a short tip, but an important one. Everyone knows that faxes are the method of choice for inter-departmental communication among anthropologists. There is nothing like that sweet sound of the fax machine booting up and aligning that paper. The delicious sound of the dialtone, beeps, and boops of the keypad are tantalizing enough to create an ambient soundtrack in your head to fall asleep to. Sometimes we just randomly fax an image of Franz Boas over to The Psychology Department not just to remind them of their academic shortcomings, but to experience the soundscape of a truly modern miracle.

Many anthropologists are unaware that although faxes are the most prestigious form of communication, there are rules that dictate how you must present yourself to colleagues. Your fax signature should provide all the information a stranger should know about you. This includes not just your name, degree, institution of conferral, title, and address, but also each student organization you chair, each devastating book review you have written, any recent internal awards, and the title of your non-academic self-published romance novel you are currently writing. Your fax signature should be at least one-half page long for junior faculty members and at least one page for senior faculty members. This way, there is no mistake where you are coming from and the authority that you hold, at least academically speaking.

21. Give Yourself a Teaching Makeover

Being your bestest anthropologist means that you need to introspectively examine how you teach and how to find new ways to meet the needs of students. Ideally, you should focus on changing your teaching style every year otherwise you will not really have anything to write in your department review each year when it asks what your goals are for next year. That moving goalpost should remind you that the pedagogical grass is always greener on the other side of the academic calendar. Sit for a second and think of that pedagogical grass. One day you will make it to that lush turf and be able to let the sunshine drip over you. Just not this year. Next year.

We are blessed to have some of the most terrific scholars in The Anthropology Department who literally walk through fire for their students. In fact, the event known as the Faculty Firewalk went on for years before the administration found out and shut it down like a bunch of wusses. So what if Dr. Nelch's toes got a little bit disfigured? It is not like he is doing any actual digging anyway. Difficult to fathom.

Being a powerhouse faculty member means recognizing the gifts and abilities you possess and figuring out how to share them with the youths. This is done in several ways, and the following tips should help you achieve new levels of pedagogy that are simply unspeakable.

Upgrade Your High-Quality Pedagogical Technology

One of the ways to reach students is by making sure you are on the same technological level they are on. Most millennials grew up with a flip phone literally embedded in their hands. This allowed them to communicate with others in unheard-of ways like text messages. It is a good idea to learn the skill of sending a text message to your students as a way to get on their level. An example of this would be to send them a text when you wake up in the morning. Here is an example of a text message Dr. Peters sends out to students each class day around 5:30 AM on the day of each class:

This way, students get mentally prepared for anthropology when they meet later in the afternoon. They cannot take their minds off the text when it is the first thing they see in the morning. Please be cognizant of texting rates, however, as one year Dr. Peters almost blew our entire tech budget on text messages alone. Some phone plans charge up to $0.25 per message so it can get a bit pricey although the payoff is worth it.

Many of your technology needs can be met at a local Radio Shack, and make sure to go there whenever there are good deals. We would like to share a story with you that actually happened on Cyber Monday of 2020. Our faculty were camped outside of Radio Shack hoping to get a steal on a modem for the linguistics lab. At one point in time, Dr. Peters had to leave and come back. Some lady gave us the stink eye thinking he had cut in line. We pointed her out to Dr. Chubb with a silent nod and a lip point. Many are unaware that Dr. Chubb is an excellent blocker and she nearly made the ISU practice squad as an inside linebacker. We just told her to hold back and box out a little so security would not remove us from the premises. Many forget that anthropologists study the hunting habits of chimpanzees, so we know what works and what does not in the primate world.

When the doors of Radio Shack opened, a roar erupted and the crowd flooded in like a scene from a zombie movie. Total chaos filled the inside of the Radio Shack. Shoppers lit safety flares and were waving them creating a muddle of light and smoke. Someone put an 8-ball in a sock started swinging it over their head. We determined it was probably a psychology professor trying to score some goods for their department. Dr. Peters shouted "Sigmund Freud was a cokehead intellectual lightweight!" at the psychology professor as we formed a wedge to cut through the scrum.

As we forced our way toward the modems, someone knocked over the Tomagotchi display sending their eggs into a scatter across the floor. Disclaimer: we are not proud of this because they are likely all dead now. At that moment, Dr. Chubb just threw a block on the stink eye lady that was so hard she seemed to leave her shoes and be suspended in midair before crashing into a display case full of Palm pilots. It reminded us that we actually needed some more Palm Pilots for the bioanthropology lab, so we added a few to our cart.

In the end, Cyber Monday 2020 was hard-fought but our faculty managed to pick up six 56k modems for the Compaq Presarios and a few zip drives for the linguistics lab. You have to admit, there is nothing sweeter than charging that loot on the departmental p-card funded by the in-house tech grant you scored over the summer. Afterward we headed to Texas Roadhouse to tend to our wounds and cool off with some Seagram's 7. Dr. Chubb required three stitches in her left hand, but it was a small price to pay to give students the experience they deserve. In sum, go the extra mile for your students when it comes to supplying them with the best technology available. They are worth it.

Change your Lecturing Style
Astute scholars always say that lecturing is dead. Well, we are writing to say that we are astuter than those scholars because they are wrong on many levels. Those "scholars" are probably just some randos on the internet that have never heard of Margaret Mead before. Lecturing is the fundamental basis of your identity when done properly, and to do it properly, you have to let go of Power-Point. There, we said it. PowerPoint is for weak loser anthropologists who are anything but powerhouse.

If one were to take a survey of all existing anthropologists across the country, they would find that nearly 99.5% of powerhouse anthropologists use overheads and nothing more. One of the main reasons for this is because most excellent anthropologists cannot really figure out the software anyway and just end up putting untold quantities of text on each slide. We once saw a presentation at the Greater Indiana Conference on Midwest Radiocarbon Dates where a record-setting 322 words were put on a single slide. The lecturer spent about fifteen seconds on it and moved on leaving us in a state of mental exhaustion. We wondered what it might have possibly said about the astonishing radiocarbon results, but now no one will ever know.

Overhead projectors allow students to connect their visual cortex to their cerebral cortex via the use of transparencies. Transparencies provide the analog method of reading and reviewing that has been proven by educational anthropologists all over the country to enhance the student experience. Fun fact: even if you accidentally place the transparency flipped in reverse or upside down, students have still been found to have greater comprehension of the material being presented. Overheads also allow you to write directly on each transparency given you have a large departmental budget for transparency pens. We tend to use each pen for around 5-7 years and it does make the writing a little difficult to read. If students complain, we just tell them that transparency pens are not free, and they should buy their own if they really feel that way. As a word of warning when you lecture, remember that *everything* is projected on the big screen. One time Dr. Nelch pulled out a pen from his pocket and it had a hair attached to the clip. One of those hairs. It was extra cringeworthy and resulted in several complaints to the dean about ponytail hairs mistakenly being projected on screens.

During the time this was written, it was increasingly difficult to find overhead projectors for reasons unknown. We sometimes cruise Elementary School auctions or the local Elk's Club to see if they have put any out near the dumpsters. When you are on the hunt, remember that Polylux projectors are categorically the best. As this book gains in popularity and changes the face of academe, expect more overhead projectors to be produced, which will increase supply and make them more available.

Of course, overheads are only one form of pedagogy to enhance student learning. Faculty in The Anthropology Department have created an entirely new method called the *Silent Classroom Technique*. This form of lecturing is largely for upper-level courses and requires students to do all of the required readings for the day. Then, students are expected to show up to class and not say a single word from start to finish. Your role as a professor is to also not say a single word either and to simply gaze back at students with a slight grin. When you are in the classroom, think deeply about what you read for the day. Think about what other people might be thinking about in the room. Think about what Franz Boas would be thinking if he were in the room. This method of introspective analysis is what separates our powerhouse faculty and students from the less illustrious faculty and students in the country. Literally trembling just writing this.

Make Incredibly Dank Memes for your Hippyster Students

If there is one thing The Anthropology Department is known for, it is that our memes are so deliciously dank that they may cause you to fall out of your chair. We have it on good authority that a student once jumped out of a moving university van because they were so blown away by the dankness of what we posted on the Tweeters. For that reason, we do suggest being in a safe and stable environment—preferably with padding—as we yeet our dank memes into you.

Professors should be aware that the face of our student population is changing. Research by our linguistic anthropologist has shown that 98% of communication by students aged 18-22 is done by text message, HTML language, online chat rooms, or reading memes sent to one another. In fact, it is not uncommon for entire conversations to take place among Gen Z students just by emailing dank memes back and forth to one another without even writing a single word. This type of symbolic communication is unprecedented, and our linguistic anthropologist predicts that language will soon be obsolete by the year 2037.

Unfortunately, copyright laws prohibit the reproduction of our incredibly dank memes in this book. To see them in their full glory, you would have to see our Tweeters page. However, we can describe a sample of ten of them in writing and you will get the point if you just use your imagination.

Meme 1: A tan bear in an orange shirt appears to be sitting and rather bored. Next to him are the words "reduction waste". In the frame below, the bear appears to be titillated and wearing a tuxedo—his eyebrows slightly raised. Next to him is the word "debitage."

Meme 2: A man is walking down a street with a woman in blue who appears to be visibly appalled by his behavior. It is because the man is looking behind him at another smiling woman who is wearing red. The man is labeled "anthropologists", whereas the angry woman is labeled "bitcoin" and the smiling woman is labeled "yamcoin."

Meme 3: A president appears in a photo with wild orange hair. His skin is even more orange and even has different levels of orange contrasting the face from the hairline. The picture is labeled "Going to tell our students this is a Munsell 10YR page"

Meme 4: A soda machine has several selections of drinks. One of the selections is "19th-century biological determinism" and the other reads "sociobiology". A hand reaches in and presses the two of the buttons to fill their drink. The hand reads "evolutionary psychology."

Meme 5: A friendly paperclip is knocking on your screen. It is asking you a question. The question is, "It looks like you are writing about an anthropology topic you don't understand. Would you like to make a spurious generalization about evolution, gender, race, or the pyramids?"

Meme 6: A header reads "When your student turns in a paper on the life of Frank Boaz." A young Anakin stares with tears welling in his eyes and suddenly clenches his jaw in a fit of rage.

Meme 7: An elderly woman walks down a path with a walker. She is labeled with "psychology is such an amazing discipline." A younger woman assisting her is labeled "sure grandma let's get you to bed."

Meme 8: A woman is whispering into an ear on the left side. Suddenly an arm appears with raised hair and goosebumps. The text above the image reads "metacarpals are just foot bones of the hand."

Meme 9: A handsome man in an oversized orange puffer coat is very offended by what is written in the frame next to him. It reads "parallel cousins". In the next frame, he is very happy, grinning with joy pointing to the frame that reads "cross cousins." This dank meme is meant as dating advice for anthropologists.

Meme 10: A red puppet is making a decision between two things. One is some fruit labeled "healthy foods" and the other is a white powder labeled "powdered up animal bone." The puppet is labeled "zooarchaeologists." The puppet begins to snort the crushed-up animal bone.

Of course, this is only a sampling of what our powerhouse faculty have to offer. We often sit down and dream up incredibly dank memes for our students during our lunch breaks or on the quick stroll over to the Pak-A-Sak. To really be your bestest anthropologist, you must understand anthropology so well that you can translate it into a language your students will fully understand.

Never, Ever, Consider Your Anthropology Films Dated
When is now? It was just then. Anyone who has ever watched the

1980's space classic *Spacedballs* knows that. Although it might be considered comical, the movie *Spacedballs* and the character Mr. Helmet has a point: anything currently being said in the present is soon in the past. This means that much of what we remember is just an interpretation of what was. In a sense, cultural anthropologists are actually anthropological ethnohistorians. Think about that for a second. We just totally injected you with some dope knowledge and now you are probably questioning the reality of your subfield.

What this means is that no matter how old your anthropology films are, they can never be classified as dated because any ethnographic work is technically describing the past. As we know, the difference between the recent past and the deep past is simply a social construction, so we can no longer classify films as being dated. This means you can show whatever you would like to your students without fear of groans. Also, because you will be attending so many prestigious regional
meetings over the semester it is good to have a lineup ready for your TA to show.

The #1 rule of any anthropology movie is that it needs to be in VHS format. This should appeal to your hippyster students. If it is in any other format, it is not worth showing and you should immediately break it into pieces with a hammer and throw it in the trashcan. Can you imagine having the budget for a DVD player in these uncertain times? Forget about it. In reality, there are really only a few good anthropology films available, and those include *Ongka's Big Moka*, *Trobriand Cricket*, *The Shackles of Tradition*, and *American Tongues*. As a word of warning, there is an alternate version of *American Tongues* that we found locked in Dr. Nelch's lower drawer. We accidentally showed that version to a class full of freshmen and nearly got sued into oblivion. Also, *American Tongues* has a racial slur in it, so maybe you should scratch that one, or just cough loudly on the yam you are snacking on as a distraction. We like *The Shackles of Tradition* the best because it has the actual voice of Franz Boas in it. Not sure how they got him on a tape recorder so early in his career, but maybe they borrowed one from the linguistics lab. It also talks about how he died in Claude Levi-Strauss's arms which has special significance if you are wearing Claude Squads. Come to think of it, maybe it was the French Structuralism that killed him.

If you are doing anthropology correctly, each student will graduate having seen these films a minimum of 14 times each. They will have them nearly memorized and even remember some of the pig's names from *Ongka's Big Moka*. We liked Phil the best. We would like to think he was quite critical to the moka exchange, but then again, there were a lot of pigs in the film.

22. Use Your Teaching Evaluations to Enhance Feelings of Self-Worth

Teaching evaluations are the critical link between you and your students and are an essential part of pedagogy. In many ways, it is a unique system of trust where you "entrust" a 18- or 19-year-old to say something that may make or break your career. Really the goal is not so much being a good teacher-scholar, but just *figuring out ways for them to like you*. One way to be very well-liked is to just toss out "A"s as if they were t-shirts at a school pep rally. You can put balled-up pieces of paper that just say "A" on them in one of those water balloon launchers and just fling them at students as they enter the class on your final day. May sure to yell out "'A's for daaaays!" if you do this because it really helps with your likeability.

However, it is entirely possible that there might be some bellyachers in the class that simply will not like you no matter how many impressions of Margaret Mead you do. This can be difficult for a lot of anthropologists because deep down we know we are amazing, and the students are just incredibly wrong for not recognizing it. Thus, our faculty have devised a foolproof method to still use student evaluations to enhance your teaching effectiveness by feeling really good about yourself.

Once you receive your teaching evaluations at the end of the semester, the best way to sort them is by those that are positive and those that are negative. Now, simply throw away the negatives in the recycling bin because...let's face it...they were kind of negative. Next, select the ones that are the most shining, beaming, and obsequious and re-read them several times over. You may even want to hang one on your wall for a bit. We recommend posting snippets of them on social media: add them to the Facebook or Tweeters, and perhaps mention that you are literally blown away by your teaching evaluations this semester. This way, other anthropologists will shake with jealous rage when they see how much you are liked, and how your freshman class described you as "legendary" or "genius." If you do not have social media, feel free to simply tape some of the snippets on your office door for other faculty to see. Remember: teaching evaluations are there for you to make improvements to your sense of self-worth and nothing more. To think otherwise is difficult to fathom.

23. When in Doubt, Call Security

If something is wrong in the academic world, do not hesitate to call security on the offenders. This can include campus security, mall security, conference security, or even Texas Roadhouse security. We propose a method of handling disputes that could best be described in anthropological language as "mediation" which can be considered binding. If someone is wrong, you need to correct it, and the best way is to get a third party involved to agree with you, which is generally a security officer. Of course, this strategy can be a double-edged sword because we have had security called on our faculty for various reasons.

Campus security can be called for most academic disputes. For example, one time one of our bioanthropologists got belligerently drunk on Seagram's 7 and began insisting that there was no obstetrician's dilemma. She was insisting that we should really be calling it the obstetrician's quandary. Another bioanthropologist confronted her saying such a discussion was foolish, and that it should best be described as the obstetrician's predicament. Strange *ad hoc* props were being used, like an orange representing a hominin head and a donut representing a pelvic bowl. Things were getting really heated and dirty looks were being given by students in the campus dining hall. Campus security was called and both bioanthropologists made their case. In the end, campus security decided that it should be called the obstetrician's quandary because it sounded much cooler and that few words actually start with the letter "q." Thus, from here we only accept the phrase *obstetrician's quandary* and anything else is simply wrong or ignorant. There was also another major dispute involving conference security at the 2019 AAPA meetings regarding the pronunciation of a hominin species. This will be covered in the next section.

Campus security can also be called for egregious mistakes, typically those made by students and sometimes faculty. For example, once a student asked if they could do a paper on the economic behavior of bands. The professor approved the topic and later in the semester, the professor received a paper on the finances of Dave Matthews. Campus security was immediately called and the student was removed from the premises. Another time, we called campus security on a forensics student who successfully identified a capitate and neglected to do a Darth Vader impression. That student was also removed from the classroom.

Faculty are also prone to making mistakes and are subject to the same treatment. We once called campus security on someone who did not begin their e-mail with "In these uncertain times..." Can you imagine doing something so foolish and asinine? Another ugly confrontation happened when one of our faculty actually advised a student to take an introductory psychology class to fill a missing Gen Ed credit on their schedule. Upon hearing the news, we became so disgusted we actually insisted the faculty member be escorted out in handcuffs. Droves of faculty members chanted "shame!...shame!...shame!" as they were paraded around campus.

Occasionally, Texas Roadhouse security has been called on our faculty for various reasons, sometimes deserved, sometimes not. One semester after The Anthropology Department received a large in-house grant for a new dot matrix printer, our faculty

THE ANTHROPOLOGY DEPARTMENT

went out to celebrate. As the night progressed, things were getting a little wild as usual. Dr. Nelch thought it would be a good idea to clear some tables out in the middle of the main room to start an anthropology dance party. He began twerking with such fervor we thought he was going to dislocate his hip. Sweat was running down his back in such massive quantities it began dripping off the frayed edges of his jean shorts like melting denim icicles. At this point, patrons were not amused, and someone must have called restaurant security. When they showed up, Dr. Nelch just started shouting, *"BACK OFF, STEAK PIGS!"* and continued twerking even while being led out with his hands zip-tied to his ankles. Difficult scene to watch, but you have to admit he probably had it coming.

Just remember, if it is an academic debate you risk losing, or if someone just forgot to log out of a computer in the linguistics lab, call campus security. You will not regret it, and you may even win a debate or two in the process. You're welcome.

24. Provide Truthful Advice to Students about the Anthropology Job Market

Part of being your bestest anthropologist is being truthful when undergraduates and graduates begin flooding into your program in record-setting numbers. You will need to lay some knowledge on them about the job market in anthropology, and this is often a difficult conversation to have. Some basic ground rules are to be realistic, but also try not to scare them off.

They will need to know there will be a flood of prospective employers literally beating down their doors for a chance to interview them following graduation. This scenario is borderline dangerous, so when we teach students about headhunters, we need to not only talk about the Ilongot of the Philippines, but also the ruthless recruiters that exist here right in our backyard of Indiana. It is common for students to receive so many phone calls for job offers that they must permanently disconnect their cellular phone or face the psychosis of continuous ringing day and night.

Not to brag, but The Anthropology Department is so successful that we place 100% of our students in high-paying positions between $21K-$27K per year. One time a student received a job offer for a position paying $31K, exceeding the salaries of most of our faculty. This type of fortune can go to students' heads because they are unaccustomed to this influx of massive wealth. One piece of advice is to tell students to receive half of their paycheck in yamcoin to socially ground them. Above all, it is important they do not forget about their humble beginnings as they literally launch their careers into space.

25. Get Literally Excited About Anthropology

Finally, our last tip for professional development involves the emotional state you should attempt to cultivate when you anthropology. If we look back at the founding of the Midwest Paradigm, there is one thing that Indiana-born Franz Boas should inspire in all of us: literal excitement. You need to get literally excited about anthropology to be your bestest anthropologist. This means you need to get a little wild. Take your hair out of the ponytail. Throw away the scrunchy. Hoot it up. Get some of those birthday horns and blow them. Every day is your birthday if you are an anthropologist.

We at The Anthropology Department are known for our celebrations that are led by both faculty and students. As a word of advice, you should be celebrating all things that are good and totally awesome. If you give an amazing lecture, encourage your students to explode with applause, standing on their chairs as you take a bow for giving the best lecture that day. It will feel really good for you, and you can post about it on the internets later. One year the U.S. News and World Report rated us the 433rd Best Anthropology Department in the country, two slots above where we were rated the year before. Of course, we know such ratings are just arbitrary, but nevertheless, faculty and students erupted in thunderous applause that was so ear-splitting that it could be heard as far as the student union. We immediately broke into our department song and began dabbing and flossing. A small child in a Babylon 5 shirt appeared out of nowhere and gave us a thumbs-up. In the distance, a dean grinned.

Our personal celebrations are well-known across the anthropological community. One time, Dr. Peters heard his devastating book review was accepted for publication in a prestigious regional journal. Upon hearing the news, he because so literally excited he immediately dropped to the floor and gave a Tiger-Woods-style fist pump. However, this fist pump was different than others because it simply kept going. The repeated motion was so consistent, the forearms of Dr. Peters became comically oversized as blood engorged his muscle tissue. We are talking about a Popeye-sized arm here, folks.

At one point, we became concerned and we thought of calling a medic. Instead, we decided to call Tiger Woods himself to see if he had ever had a fist pump last this long. He said he would be over right away as he just happened to be on a PGA tour at Whispering Hills. In an hour, Mr. Tiger showed up and instead of helping, immediately dropped to his knee and started Tiger-Woods-style fist pumping. Upon seeing this electric atmosphere, students, faculty, and staff also dropped to their knees and started Tiger-Woods-style fist pumping in unison. No one really knows what happened after that. It is likely everyone just blacked out in ecstasy. When we awoke, Mr. Tiger was gone, but a mysterious note was left on Lucy's desk that said the following:

"Never stop pumping. -T."

Take these words of wisdom with you. Never pass up the opportunity to celebrate something about yourself or others. Only when you reach this level of anthropologist will the haters begin to love, and the jealous become altruistic. In other words, never stop pumping. We wish a safe recovery for Mr. Tiger and hope we can pump with him again in the future. This leads us to our next section which includes some advice for each of the subdisciplines.

SECTION FOUR: DISCIPLINE-SPECIFIC ADVICE

"Anthropology is the most humanistic of the neat disciplines, and the most fun of the scientific disciplines"

-THE ANTHROPOLOGY DEPARTMENT

The purpose of this section is to provide you with a few tidbits of information concerning your subdiscipline and beyond. Although each tip may not specifically relate to your field, take a moment to read all of them in case you need to totally own some n00b at the latest conference.

26. Do Not Lend Anything to a Forensic Anthropologist

Everyone knows a forensic anthropologist and what they do in their spare time. We realize some forensic anthropologists mainly study bones, but then there is that other brand of forensic anthropologists. You know, the ones you kind of...*worry about.* Yes, we are talking about the drippy forensic anthropologist types that like all the soft tissue stuff and will never stop talking about it at departmental gatherings and holiday parties. They are the ones you should never lend anything to, and we will tell you why in a moment.

So about these drippy types...it is not that they are not nice people, they just make you kind of *wonder* a bit. Like, why? How did you get so deeply engrossed in this field? Please do not say Bones otherwise we will put in an anonymous FBI tip on you immediately. We are literally trying to see this from your perspective, folks. Faculty tried watching beetles decompose a body and were not able to even get through the first thirty seconds of the Nine Inch Nails music video. We once took a tour of a body farm thinking it would be kind of happy like Green Acres but with corpses. It ended up looking like one of those horrific scenes from the end of Poltergeist where all the bodies started coming out of the ground. We cannot unsee that. We know you cannot either, and that is why we just kind of *wonder*.

This leads us to the main point of this tip concerning the lending of items to forensic anthropologists. It was the fall semester of 1992 and Right Said Fred was all the rage. We were having a fall departmental gathering for the students and faculty and Dr. Nelch offered to bring in some of his famous slow-cooked meatballs to feed the masses. The party was rocking as usual, and Dr. Nelch was occasionally slipping back to his office to take a few swings of Seagram's 7 from his upper desk drawer. After a while, it was apparent that Dr. Nelch had too much, and was no longer able to rollerblade home safely. We suggested he leave his crockpot in the department as he walked home to sleep it off. At the end of the party, our forensic anthropologist offered to clean everything up and casually asked whether they should bring the crockpot home. Faculty agreed.

Over the next few months, several new type specimens began to arrive at the forensics lab. They were newly cleaned human bone from a recently donated cadaver that our forensic anthropologist was quite proud of. "The students will really be able to learn from these!" they exclaimed. This went on for some time until Dr. Nelch casually mentioned getting his crockpot back to make another batch of his famous meatballs. Our forensic anthropologist looked a little blindsided, and responded with, "of course!" The crockpot came back to the department, and unfortunately, no new type specimens never came in after that. We will never know what delicious recipes our forensic anthropologist was cooking in the crockpot, but presumably they were making some great food to pass the time as they boiled their bones at home.

Thus, you should never lend anything to a forensic anthropologist because clearly they take a long time to return things. You really should not have to ask a person for your crockpot back. The good news from this story is that Dr. Nelch now has his crockpot, and is ready to make his famous meatballs for the holiday party in December. We are really looking forward to them because they are extra tasty.

27. Learn to Pronounce "Denisovan" Correctly and Win Poetry Contests

If there is one thing that is a hallmark of being your bestest anthropologist, it is that you are able to not only pronounce obscure anthropological names correctly, you also make the effort to make sure that others pronounce them correctly too. Did you know that four out of every five hominin species names are mispronounced and the general public does not even know it? Of course, we are talking about the biggie. The one that every television program and person you encounter seems to pronounce incorrectly no matter how hard they try. That species is *H. denisova,* also known as the Denisovans.

To the untrained eye, many would see the word Denisovan and find the pronunciation relatively straightforward: dɪˈniːsovən or "den-i-so-van." However, our linguistic anthropologist took some time off from researching memespeak and tracked down the history of its origins. It turns out that the original discoverer of the first fossils wanted it to be pronounced dɪˈniːshovən or "den-i-sho-van."

You probably just trembled a bit. That is OK, because we did too. We considered these data to be so revolutionary, we actually got in the LeSabre and drove 27 hours to the 2019 AAPA meetings in Cleveland to spread the word. We were met with outright hostility. Some members actually accused us of trying to sound elitist and even like Sean Connery. At one point in the evening on March 30th, several faculty became belligerent and nearly started a fistfight in the hotel lobby. We immediately called conference security and they sided with our faculty. Case closed.

Since that fateful evening, many scholars have been reluctant to change their pronunciation of Denisovan, but we have made some headway into various avenues. One such inroad was through poetry—specifically limericks—that create a means to capture the public imagination. In fact, we once wrote a limerick about Denisovans that was voted the best anthropology limerick *of all time* by the American Anthropological Association. Take a moment and soak in how incredible this limerick actually was:

> There once was a bioanth joven
> Who saw *Homo* as interwoven
> To settle a farce
> He decided to parse:
> It's actually pronounced "den-i-sho-van"

Literally shaking right now. Perhaps it is just the beauty of the words as they flow across the page into your mind. Or maybe it is the fact that it indeed won the best anthropology limerick of all time according to the American Anthropological Association and won $100. We know it was not a yamcoin payout, but it was still one of the most fantastic moments in the history of our department. Faculty high fived and dabbed. A small child in the Babylon 5 shirt smiled. The results came in overwhelmingly in our favor:

Weeks later we received a beautiful hand-written note from the AAA that Lucy still keeps on the department message board to this day. When we need a little boost before teaching a class, we simply look up to it and feel the tremendous energy radiating into our souls:

In sum, if you are going to be the bestest anthropologist you can be, make sure to be incredibly accurate about the pronunciation of hominin species. Have your linguistic anthropologist dig up the facts, present those facts at conferences to your peers, write earth-shattering limericks, and win international contests. The academic community will be better off, and you might even have $100 more in your pocket to spend on your next trip to Texas Roadhouse.

28. Run the Greatest Archaeology Field School

As mentioned above, if you are a North American archaeologist, you should ideally have a field site picked out no further than a nickel traced on a map around your hometown. Remember, convenience is what matters, not your research questions. You are about to run the greatest field school that has ever been run. It will be so legendary that students will reference it to the day they die and forget that you took advantage of their cheap labor. The following is a plan for you to follow for a standard four-week dig. So slap on your jorts, and start getting disturbingly tan. Here are some tips for the greatest field school!

The Setup

That archaeology lab is not going to clean itself. There are things in there that are so old we are not sure if they belong in an antique store or some hippyster bodega in Indianapolis. We here there are a lot of hippysters in that city. Honestly, we do not even know where these things even came from. Items just appear in the archaeology lab and simply sit in perpetuity in the steamy 87-degree climate until they collect so much dirt they can no longer be recognized. We *think* that is a stuffed squirrel holding a Schlitz beer with a fake cigarette hanging out of his mouth, but we are not sure if it is a weasel. Your field school is the perfect opportunity to get some things cleaned that you were never able to get to because you were busy publishing devastating book reviews.

You should plan on devoting at least an entire week to spiffing up the lab before you get started on your dig. That means lifting every single deteriorated cardboard box and moving it out from the wall before deciding to put it back because you do not want to deal with what is inside. Students should be prepared to use push brooms and even some of the excavation equipment itself to help clean up in the lab. Use it as an opportunity to teach the students about stratigraphy as you go through yellowed layers of reports that were never published and Cheeto wrappers that date to at least 1977. WARNING: there is a chance you might stumble on a retired archaeologist's skin bin, and if that happens you may have to simply burn down the lab for insurance money and ask the students to never speak of it again. Difficult to unsee that. People just looked *different* back then.

Take special caution with rusty tools because they might give your students tetanus. One time we were worried that a student got tetanus from a sharp trowel, but it turned out they were just kind of a mouthbreather. Students even made a fun game to toss kernels of popcorn into his mouth when he was not looking. They called it the "Ross Toss" because the student's name was Ross and he really liked popcorn. Once your lab is spiffed up, it is time to think of some of the other logistical concerns associated with a field project.

Your Field Vehicle
The department's LeSabre might not be large enough to haul your students to and from campus, so you are going to have to sweet talk maintenance into letting you borrow one of the GMC vans they have in the back of the building. It might be school policy that the department has to pay for the rental, but we have found that if you take a crisp $20 bill and drop it next to Larry, you can simply say, "oops looks like you dropped something Larry!" He will accidentally drop the van keys somewhere near the vehicle later that day. One time they ended up in a storm drain, but if this happens, remember that students are quite nimble and can easily fit down there.

The GMC vans from maintenance are amazing field vehicles because they still have original shocks, tires, and consoles from at least 1983. This means that simply driving to the field site is an unforgettable experience as you are filled with the vivacious terror that the van may fall apart on the highway. Most of the vehicles have rusted wheel wells, so if the windshield is too cracked to see clearly, you can always have a student poke their head into the wheel well to make sure your lane placement is OK. Just as a heads-up, the GMC vans do have a tendency to fishtail even in good conditions, so if you are off-roading up or down a hill, steer into the fishtail. Remember that the van is going to get dirty with all the shovels and screens, but this should not be an issue because there is already a fine layer of mud on the floorboards of the vehicle. Sometimes we just take it to the SuperWash, roll the windows down, and let it do its thing.

Mapping your excavation area
Being a world-class archaeologist means having an accurate map of your field site. If you are a Midwest Archaeologist, this more than likely means you will be located in a flat farm field with corn or soybeans. It is your duty to make sure that every single inch of that site is mapped out even though you know it has been plowed for years. Hopefully, you managed to find your total station or theodolite if your students cleaned out your lab. Here comes the tricky part: finding out how it works. You will likely spend a good four days puzzling over your total station, forgetting to charge the battery, or trying to get it out of Estonian language prompts. You will spend an extra day or two figuring out how to level it. You will curse the inventors of the total station for their mere existence. You will wonder why it does not have a compass attached to it, and why you failed to bring yours for that day. You will estimate where north is, ignore the lean of the total station, and just flipping call it a day.

The actual mapping of the site is quite fun for students, and they will soon learn to use the total station in a professional capacity. This means practicing using it as a mock laser weapon and trying to zap friends in the eye when they least expect it. Hilarity will ensue, and student accuracy will be improved over time using this playful game. One of our retired archaeologists used to do this all the time where he challenged students to zap him in the face as a means of practice. He would crawl through the soybeans, pop his head up, and yell "duck hunt!" Unfortunately, he had to retire a while back due to eyesight issues. It is tragic because he probably had bad genes or did not eat enough carrots. Guess we will never know. Students will also begin to experience the sensation of holding a stadia rod. Did you know it is a scientifically proven fact that the time-space continuum slows when holding a stadia rod? Five actual seconds of holding a stadia rod is exactly equal to five hours for the holder. Let that sink in: stadia rod holders actually age at different time intervals than their non-stadia-rod-holding peers. If you ever go to the Upper Midwestern Conference on Soil Changes you can definitely pick out the stadia-rod-holders in the crowd.

The next task is to lay in the units using a standard archaeological measuring length of trowels. It only makes sense that trowels are a standard unit of measurement because they are always available to archaeologists and are super accurate. We are not talking about any trowel either: Marshalltown only. None of the Fiskars trash. A good unit size to start with is either a three by three trowel or a six-by-six trowel unit. You can use the total station to mark off each of the units according to the cardinal directions as your students line up trowels to get the correct distances. This will take you three days.

Excavating

Everyone knows you cannot let a 19- or 20-year-old just start digging at an archaeological site. They could do something really bad and mess up your perfect contexts irreparably. Even digging into a plow zone could have enormous impacts down the road, and you need to teach them how to recognize soil zone can change the subtle features associated with Midwest Archaeology. For this reason, you will need to put your hair back into a ponytail, scoot those jorts over to the nearest unit, and start showing the students how to dig.

For the first two days, you will want to show students how to remove the humus layer. You are free to make any joke you wish about not having enough pita chips or saltines at this moment. One time Dr. Nelch actually brought some pita chips to the site and ate part of the humus layer just as a gag. On a side note, he was treated for *E.coli* the following day because apparently there were cattle in the area. To train students to be wonderful archaeologists you must teach them to respect the humus layer as you are never sure what you will find there. We have found pull tabs for aluminum cans and even a fragment of a tractor wheel once. That was really exciting. Remember to keep those section walls straight!

For the next two days, you will want to train students on

how to spot soil changes. It can be really tricky because it means that soil is a different color than another soil. It can tell you a lot about prehistory though, especially distinguishing between the humus layer and the next. You just do not know it yet! You can spend another day teaching students how to screen dirt and separate artifacts from non-artifacts. If you are a seasoned professional archaeologist, you may just want to save everything anyway because it is difficult to trust 19- to 20-year-olds.

Return to the lab

You know what they say: each day digging in the field requires double that time in the lab! Because you were digging for five days, you will spend the next ten days in the lab with students analyzing what you learned. Make sure to backfill any of the humus layer that you removed and collect any artifacts that came out of this layer. For the next ten days, meticulously analyze what came out of your units. Have the students illustrate the artifacts, even if that means learning to draw a button or a nail several times over.

At the end of the lab session, have the students write up a report. Your field school report will go straight into the filing cabinet in the lab for a future archaeologist to find. It will be yellow by that point, but you will live in eternity for your unforgettable four-week field school. By that time you will have presented your results at several prestigious regional meetings, and you may even win a paper award or two. You're welcome.

29. Bioarchaeologists Should Have Their Bones Studied by Future Bioarchaeologists

We just think it is fair. If you built your career off someone else's bones, someone should be able to build their career off yours. With any luck, you may end up in a box somewhere on campus in perpetuity, which is an ultimate honor for any powerhouse professional who dedicated their life to the discipline.

30. Practice Thicc Description

Did you know the orangutans have a predisposition for obesity? This means they can sometimes grow larger than individuals from Collegeville, who apparently also have a predisposition for obesity. We know there are good evolutionary reasons that orangutans tend to pack on the pounds in their spare tire, and we should seek to understand the reasons as researchers.

Thus, if you are a primatologist you may want to pick up a cutting-edge topic in anthropology: thicc description. It is definitely cool and hip for the youths because "thicc" is a slang word for "thick." Our linguistic anthropologist has actually figured out a phonological distinction between the two spellings. She spent several days interviewing youthful students to figure out the semantic and pragmatic contexts of the word. She found it could be used in combination with the word "boi" as in "thicc boi," but this was usually in reference to an animal that is a hecking chonker. For example, an obese cat can be a thicc boi but not necessarily a human. It can also be paired with "AF," which we assume is a shortening of "as fun," because being thicc can also be a lot of fun. Just as a side note, apparently walking up to strangers asking "what does being thicc mean to you?" can be subject to some gross misinterpretations. Lots of dirty looks have been given to our linguist, so we just thought you might want to know in case you do your own thicc description.

Back to the orangutans: research on primate obesity is classic thicc description. It is so much better than that time Clifford Geertz crashed some town's cockfight and then crammed a bunch of innuendo into his recollection of the event. He probably should have been arrested by Balinese police just for titling it "Deep Play." Seriously thinking of putting in an anonymous CIA tip right now as we write this. Orangutans do not really mind if you call them thicc, and in fact often enjoy it when you compliment them on their gargantuan cheek pouches while describing them. In fact, it is not the worst idea in the world to become thicc enough yourself so it appears you have cheek pouches too. Our primatologist finds that it helps establish trust between the researcher and subject. Our faculty have definitely encountered a few people at Texas

Roadhouse with cheek pouches and we just assumed they were the dominant males/females. A final piece of advice: the hip and youthful students will love you if you practice thicc description. You may even plan a field school in Thighland.

31. Do Not Ever Look in the Locked Drawer of a Cultural Anthropologist

Seriously, what are those video cassettes even of? Why would the drawer need to be locked? Also, why is there always a 1970s-era couch in the office of every cultural anthropologist? Let us hope this is all unrelated.

stares at Dr. Peters

32. Find a Way to Make Steven Pinker Block You

For being such a proponent of the enlightenment, you would think that someone would not really care about what is said about them on the Tweeters. Apparently, true freedom of thought means you can simply turn off other people's freedom of thought so you can just think in your head of all the lame evolutionary psychology interpretations you have (for more about psychology, please see *Tip 35: Sigmund Freud Was a Cokehead Intellectual Lightweight*). Evolutionary psychology is just so basic in its tautological premise that it sounds like something developed in the 1800s. In fact, we once proposed a nationwide cancellation of student loan debt, except for evolutionary psychology majors because they can probably just retroactively explain their way out of it.

This leads us to Steven Pinker, who apparently has been pretty heavy-handed with the block button. In fact, many of the followers of The Anthropology Department have been blocked by Mr. Steven. One has to wonder how he took the time to do all of this. Did he use an autoblock chain program like that one crazy lady who suggested all academics were bots? Who was that person again? We will never know. Plot twist: she was probably a bot all along just learning to love. Believe it or not, were blocked by Mr.

Steven for a single tweet:

We may never know how this happened, but apparently all variants of his name are off-limits to academic scrutiny. Thus, we encourage you to find a creative way to make Steven Pinker block you. There is definitely a plus side to this. You probably did not really want to hear his insights about evolutionary psychology, why Enlightenment-influenced imperialism was not all bad, or how women might be less-suited for representation at elite universities due to biological differences. You also probably do not want to hear he received funding from that one guy who didn't kill himself. Note this is all true.

In a sense, this reminds us of the time our faculty watched *Strangest Things* for the first time and uncovered some amazing metaphorical allegories hidden within the subplot of the series: Will Byers is like anthropology, and Barb is like evolutionary psychology because no one in the community really cares when Barb disappears.

33. Never Get Between Two Fire-Breathing Mayanists

Everyone knows Mayanists have not really done fieldwork in

years. In fact, even the thought of touching a trowel when they were doing fieldwork probably sends a shiver down their spines. We have it on good authority most of their excavations were done by local workers, and they only picked up trowels for the pictures or documentarians. For all we know, they were probably sitting in the bodega throughout the day nipping on cheap rum or tequila, which is largely because Seagram's 7 is tough to come by down there without bribing a customs agent. This slow daily pickling is what allows Mayanist to live long lives despite the tough conditions and hazards of living in Central America or Yucatan. In fact, the mean life expectancy of Mayanists is estimated to be 105 years and they often do not require embalming following death.

Many Mayanists are legendary for reasons unknown. Maybe they found a cool artifact once in 1970 and had it printed in the local Collegeville bulletin? Not really sure, but as a tip to anthropologists everywhere: Mayanists are as prickly as they are prestigious. Luckily, most of the time it will not be directed at you. Mayanists breathe more fire at one another than that show Lord of the Thrones. They just seem to hate each other so much for reasons unknown. Maybe it is because the other Mayanist found a tomb in 1973? Or maybe it is because one of them got an inexplicable grant for millions of dollars to fly lasers over a site and make a pretty map? We will never really know the real reasons, but here is a tip: never get between two fire-breathing Mayanists. Just let them duke it out at faculty meetings and try not to meet their gaze. We once saw a Mayanist jump across a table and suplex another Mayanist just for suggesting Olmecs were the mother culture of Mesoamerica. It is likely they deserved it, but still you do not want to be on the receiving end of a fire-breathing Mayanist's suplex when they get salty. You're welcome.

34. Brush Up on Facts About Hominin and Extinct Apes

Everyone loves a good hominin fact, and such facts are an amazing way to get conversations going at holiday parties or piano recitals. One time Dr. Chubb was able to corner a complete stranger

BEING YOUR BESTEST ANTHROPOLOGIST

at a Bar Mitzvah for 125 minutes straight just by feeding them amazing facts about the difference between robust and gracile australopithecines. We are certain the rabbi appreciated all of the information and was a real sport about it. If you are willing to become the bestest anthropologist, you should know the history of our hominin brethren front-and-back, and that means being able to communicate facts that are easily digested by the general public.

One thing to keep in mind is that many hominin and early primates were named for the characteristics they had, or by what researchers were actively doing at the time. Let us take a look at a non-hominin Miocene ape, Oreopithecus, that roamed what is modern-day Italy. Many think that the name Oreopithicus derives from the Greek roots of "hill-ape," but they are terribly mistaken and should probably leave the discipline after thinking such nonsense.

To understand the nomenclature of this amazing extinct ape, you must look to the relationship of the National Biscuit Company (A.K.A. "Nabisco") and Louis Leakey in 1933. Louis had just attended trade school and had several failed starts beginning his own business in plumbing. Apparently the name of his business, "Leakey Plumbing," failed to catch on, likely due to a lack of creativity and overall shoddy workmanship. Young Louis decided to switch his gaze to our human history and study paleoanthropology. In 1933, the worldwide depression was in full swing, and several corporations were looking for ways to market their products creatively. At the time, there were several obscure ape fossils found in Italy that went by the species name *Hydroxus wilesis.*

Here's where things get strange. It is well known that young Louis Leakey was quite the cookie man. He often bought hundreds of boxes of cookies just to keep at his desk as he studied, often creating stacks of cookies to memorize represent different Epochs. He would then eat entire stacks using a specialized chute he designed. "If you don't do the work, you can't have the cookie," Louis used to say. In 1933, the works of Louis were noted by the National Biscuit Company who approached him about naming rights of a species. Noting the success of cookies during the great depression, Louis thought about the great wealth they could create, so naturally he thought the name should include a reference to riches, particularly gold. He envisioned a golden Miocene ape eating cookies with a baby deer looking on as a powerful marketing image, and suggested the Spanish word *oro* be incorporated into a species name to replace the obscure *Hydroxus wilesis*. Thus, the name *Oropithicus bambolli* was suggested, meaning "Golden Ape with Bambi." Sensing a hit, he submitted the name to several publishers, and they retroactively agreed to scrub any reference to *Hydroxus wilesis* and replace it with *Oropithicus bambolli.* However, in a strange stroke of error, a typo in the original letter added an extra "e," which is why we have "Oreopithicus" used throughout most of the literature today. Feel free to share this story with professionals at your next academic conference to really wow them with your insider knowledge.

35. Sigmund Freud Was a Cokehead Intellectual Lightweight

That one really caught your attention. Here at The Anthropology Department, we are deeply concerned with students who are interested in psychology. As mentioned previously, we have the poster of the kitty that says "Hang in There! Don't Major in Psychology!" on our office wall. We have even called campus security on our own faculty member for merely suggesting that an advisee take a psychology course. Furious just typing that.

Part of the reason for this disgust lies with the founder of psychoanalysis, Sigmund Freud. Why does everyone even like that guy anyway? Is it because he thought it would be cool to talk about dreams while obliterated on cocaine? Dr. Nelch's cousin does that all the time, and it is not like we give him a major intellectual platform. At our last holiday party, he said that he had a dream that the shovel guy in Home Alone was actually Jesus. Sounds pretty much like a Freudian argument to us: a load of absolute nonsense dreamed up by someone who just ingested a baggy of the devil's dandruff.

Maybe people like Sigmund Freud because he sees penises in everything and everyone. Is that why? So someone can have a giggle in High School about saying "penis," and then arrange the beanbags and skinny bookshelf in the classroom so it looks like a giant penis with beanbag testes? Does that make people laugh? Maybe it does, but it is not as funny as a yam joke. In fact, this kind of performance-art-inspired penis joke is as weak as Sigmund Freud's CV. We browsed through Freud's CV the other day and found he never even wrote a devastating book review in his life. Difficult to fathom.

We at The Anthropology Department can also debunk a key Freudian theory: no one has penis envy. This was especially apparent when an unknown person thought it would be "funny" to put their penis in our Xerox machine and leave the copies in random books around the office. We are still finding the disturbing images to this day, and that happened 31 years ago. No one envies it. In fact, we do not like it one bit. Theory disproven, Mr. Freud. Checkmate.

Really though, is it because Freud had a weird fixation with his mom? We have it on good authority that Sigmund Freud's mom was not even that hot, and kind of looked like Janet Reno. There are plenty of anthropologists that are infinitely more attractive, but no one really seems to lust after them. In fact, Dr. Chubb has not been on a date in 27 years despite having a truly beautiful anthropological mind. Let us step back and think about this one, why would a researcher think all of our children are incestuous parent-killers? Sounds like something someone dreamed up after ripping a giant speedball of foo-foo dust.

But seriously, Sigmund Freud was a cokehead intellectual lightweight who never wrote a devastating book review in his life. If you read about his life, you will find he spent copious amounts of time with someone named "Little Hans." Who is this Little Hans one might ask? It turns out Little Hans was *a five year old boy who had a phobia of horses and wanted to play with his "widdler."* Sorry folks, if we are going to hang out with anyone, it would be someone named Little Franz. He likes horses and keeps it in his pants. You should too.

36. Your Linguistic Anthropology Degree is Worthless Unless You Use It for Beatboxing

It is a known fact that linguistic anthropologists are the most popular anthropologists due to their dope beatboxing skills. This is a really good thing because it shows people can look past the drab clothing, knee-length socks, and permanently mounted tape recorders on the belts of many linguistic anthropologists.

When you think about it, linguistic anthropologists have been training for beatboxing their entire lives. After all, why would anyone on earth be remotely interested in learning all of those phonemes if they were not going to put them to good use? One time Lucy once thought one of our linguistic anthropologists was having a stroke in their office. The faculty all rushed down the hallway to assist. When we broke down the door with a fire extinguisher, we found Dr. Jeffers just had an International Phonetic Alphabet on her desk and was really going to town on it.

If it is one thing that students really love, it is a linguistic anthropologist that can beatbox. It definitely appeals to the youths because they enjoy the "hip-hop culture" that has long been associated with anthropology. Dr. Jeffers has some really sick flow as she lays down fly voiceless glottalic eggresives with ejective stops. She was once involved in a beatboxing battle at Texas Roadhouse where she got extra crunk on the microphone. She yeeted a series of ingressive bilabial trills and apical closures until her challenger gave up. That person has never been seen again, and we assume they just moved away from Indiana after suffering such an enormous and humiliating defeat on the big stage.

Another time during open mic night at Texas Roadhouse, Dr. Jeffers crashed some nectar rhymes that literally brought the house down. In the middle of beatboxing some pulmonic ventricular phonations, she broke into an acapella rendition of O.P.P. that was totally on fleek. She actually got a filthy call-and-response going with the audience where she shouted, "You down with Anthro-G?!!" and patrons responded, "Yeah you know me!" At the end of the performance, she was carried off the stage by engorged diners who were stunned by the popping fresh beats that were just laid down upon them.

You may be surprised to hear that some truly famous people have recognized the beatboxing skills of our linguistic anthropologists. For example, Dax Shepard, famous anthropologist and star of *Without a Paddle*, once recognized our rich tradition of departmental beatboxing:

Literally in ecstasy just sharing this amazing memory. You could be us. You just need to brush up on your phonemes and beatboxing skills and get to your local Texas Roadhouse. You will not regret it, and your students will love you.

SECTION FIVE: SPREADING THE JOY OF ANTHROPOLOGY

"There is a way to get rich in anthropology. It is in the followers you make."

-FRANZ BOAS, COLLEGEVILLE, 1888

Congratulations on making it this far. Your transformation into your bestest anthropologist is nearly complete as your transition stage draws to a close and your reincorporation stage begins. This means by the end of this chapter, your liminality will be more grounded, and you will be fully recognized as the powerhouse person you are. However, there is one last step in your journey and that is to learn how to make the pie higher. This means finding ways to spread the joy of anthropology to others that are academically destitute or otherwise lost in life. If we turn to the quote above by Indiana-born Franz Boas, we soon start to learn that anthropology is not just some silly academic topic you study to get out of doing yardwork for your grandmother. It is a lifestyle and a good one at that. Your final task of being your bestest anthropologists is to begin finding ways to spread the joy of anthropology to others. You will be yeeting that anthropology right into the public, and they will adore you for it.

37. Build Your Shrine to Franz Boas

Shrines serve as important physical features to demarcate the difference between the sacred and the profane. They serve as intense culturally charged materializations of ideology, and at times can serve to mark in-group and out-group membership. We totally looked that up in an intro textbook, but it is still super neat and you can think that we came up with it because we wrote it.

Because shrines have such cosmologically charged power, you must think about building your shrine to the big daddy of anthropology, Franz Boas. Let's just say that Boas is great because he just makes you feel good. We can go back in his writings and find the stuff that is awesome and just kind of gloss over the questionable or unethical stuff he did. After all, no one wants to be a downer or that person at a departmental function, so just shut your pie hole, everyone!

Now, building your shrine to Boas should be an execution of your interpretation of what is important, not just to Boas, but to anthropology more generally. Here at The Anthropology Department, we have one of the best shrines to Franz Boas the world has ever seen. To build our shrine, Dr. Peters got a bunch of papier-mâché from the art department and some chicken wire to build a full-size replica of a shirtless Franz Boas. He chose the classic Boasian pose: arms out, barefoot, emerging from a hula hoop with a facial expression of a pant hoot that would even make Jane Goodall proud. The end product was actually really good, and Dr. Peters finished some of the details of Boas's rock-hard abs and thirst trap mustache using a Sharpie we found in the bottom drawer of the archaeology lab.

When the statue was finished, we placed it in the empty office of a cognitive anthropologist we recently denied tenure and began to surround it with important symbolism. First, we created miniature versions of all of Boas's students using oven-baked clay: Ruth Benedict, Zora Neale Hurston, Edward Sapir, Paul Radin, and William Jones. We placed them on a model academic building behind the papier-mâché sculpture of Boas so it appears that they are looking down upon him from great academic heights. We did have an Alfred Kroeber miniature, but that got taken off the building. Next, we took headshots of all our faculty members and pasted them directly behind Boas's students. When you create

THE ANTHROPOLOGY DEPARTMENT

your shrine to Franz Boas, you may even want to create a statue of yourself to place next to him. You can fill in the background with positive teaching evaluation printouts to channel the energy (see Tip #22). It is optional to put images of Lewis Henry Morgan, Sigmund Freud, and a card that just says "ethnocentrism" under the soles of the feet of Boas so he is forever dominating them. To finish off the shrine, Dr. Peters placed a collection of yams that were carefully curated from local growers around Boas's birthplace of Collegeville at the base. The idea is that the original yam root crops would have been around the time Boas was born here, and thus via contagious magic, contain a direct vegecultural line to his energy.

When faculty or students visit our shrine to Boas, it is customary to remove your shoes and your shirt and mimic his pose as you enter the sacred space. If you feel uncomfortable doing this, it is acceptable to simply enter the shrine with a pant hoot expression on your face, but you should keep it that way the whole time just as a sign of respect. Many visitors bring yams from different parts of the world to place at the shrine or light a yam-scented candle. One of the more important offerings is to bring a small flask of seal milk to physically pour into Boas's mouth to remind him of the good times at Baffin Island. Just do not give him too much though. We all know what happens when seal milk is consumed in excess.

Our Collegeville faculty have a tradition on Boas's birthday of standing at the shrine and saluting his image for 24 hours straight. This tradition is not for the weak, as fasting must take place to not interrupt the salute. It is not uncommon to see intense visions of anthropology when performing the birthday salute. The salute has gone on for at least 78 years after the first shrine to Franz Boas was constructed by the department. It was accidentally destroyed when one of the yam candles burned a bit too hot.

For a less intensive use of the shrine, we hold an annual Franz Boas mustache contest where students and faculty try to grow the most Boasian mustache. Don't worry: this is an all-inclusive event! Dr. Johnson scored some black-market androgen pills in 1998 in case you need to kick it up a notch. To decorate for this event we put little mustaches everywhere around the department. We even put some on the bathroom mirrors so it looks like you have a little mustache as you wash your hands. Dr. Nelch even put a mustache on the 2001 LeSabre and yelled out "free mustache rides!" to passerbys as he drove around Collegeville. Unfortunately, it was only a matter of time before the authorities were called. To this day we are not sure why this happened, but maybe it is illegal to offer free rides to strangers in Collegeville.

In sum, construct your shrine to Franz Boas today, because as each day goes by, you could be offending his spirit even more. The mark of a neat anthropologist is having a great effigy, and you can design various ritual events around your newly constructed sacred space.

38. delete this section

Lucy you can just go ahead and delete this one and re-number the tips. Also Lucy, we are running low on the zip disks again in the computer lab so please order a few more. Thank you.

39. Be Mindful of Conspiracies Against the Midwest Paradigm

The Midwest Paradigm is the greatest anthropological frame of thinking ever constructed, and all other ideas fall short. Simply put, if you are using ideas that were developed outside of the Midwest, they are considered passé, outdated, and wrong. Your job of being your bestest anthropologist is to make sure this paradigm grows and blossoms inside of you, your students, your colleagues, and even gas station attendants. However, with our great fame and evangelization, there is a price. Supporters of the Midwest Paradigm have had to go underground to avoid scrutiny from other parts of the country. Jealousy abounds in both the West Coast and East Coast. Not as much in Canada because they speak French there, so they probably have not read many of our publications in prestigious regional journals.

One scholar was so well-versed in the Midwest Paradigm they had to go underground to evade an academic cabal that seeks to destroy it. This person is only known as Y. There is good reason to believe that Franz Boas himself actually entrusted important information to Y before Boas's death 89 years ago. Because of the temporal gap, we believe that the belief in the Midwest Paradigm can prolong people's lives to unnatural levels. This would explain how our anthropology faculty in Collegeville are generally elderly and unwilling to retire.

Numerous clues throughout Franz Boas's life show he had to signal to Y in a clandestine manner. Many anthropologists have heard of several unusual photos Boas, many without his clothes on. Luckily, those pictures have never been made public and were destroyed by Y after they were found in a shoebox following his death. Most anthropologists are familiar with another set of photos that were taken of Boas for the exhibit at the Smithsonian. In common belief, it is thought that the pictures were taken for a recreation of a Kwakwaka'wakw dance. However, on close inspection, some of the images were actual physical signals to Y. Note the clear reference to Y in the following images of Boas (linked due to copyright restrictions that were probably created by the cabal itself):

https://twitter.com/anthropologydp/status/1299689341644664835?s=20

Yet another:

https://twitter.com/anthropologydp/status/1299689346270982144?s=20

With each signal to Y, Franz Boas was able to pass off important notes using a trashcan in the basement of a pizzeria in the greater D.C. Metro area. Those notes would be smuggled out of the city using a complex network of anthropologists who brought the messages across the Appalachians of West Virginia, along the Ohio River, and into the great plains of northwestern Indiana.

This was all done because Midwest Paradigm was deemed too dangerous for the Eastern U.S., which had its own inferior paradigms and began to show allegiances to the inchoate academic cabal.

For those who doubt the existence of the academic cabal: take note whenever there are budget cuts at your institution. It seems that whenever the discussion of cuts arises, a Midwest anthropology lab that is only used two or three times seems to be the first on the chopping block. They almost always are deemed "not necessary," "too expensive to heat," and are slated for demolition. Coincidence? We think not. Think of the videotapes in your film room that have not been viewed in years and suddenly have to be tagged and "liquidated" because they "need to be moved for an actual faculty office." Many of those were made by Midwestern anthropologists, and now their voices are forever lost. Also, think about the prestigious local journals that you cannot access on the internets. The cabal is at work here folks to keep the Midwest Paradigm down. Literally disgusted just thinking about this.

On occasion, Y still sends us cables. We typically use those cables to hook up the VCR in the linguistics lab to view some of the video cassettes that are sent known as "Y Drops." Often the tapes are informative but quite disturbing in the scale and severity of the threats to the paradigm. They feature Y with graduation robes draped over their head, using a child's toy voice changer to hide their identity. Occasionally, someone interrupts Y to bring in a plate of yam brownies and some seal milk. This makes us wonder what the identity of Y really is.

Perhaps we have said too much.

winks in anthropologist

40. Dr. Peters May Have Dated Your Mom

This is simply meant to be an informative declaration, and we thought you should know. No further action needs to be taken at this time.

41. Get Stormy Daniels to Give You a Bump

Did you know that we are the only anthropology department in the entire world (and by extension, universe) that is followed by Stormy Daniels on the Tweeters?

Yes, that Stormy. If you do not believe it, just go and look. We will wait.

Now that you have confirmed, we just want to say that getting some celebrity backing is the best thing you can do to help launch yourself on the international stage. We have a jovial relationship with Ms. Stormy and sometimes send each other funny things. She makes us laugh, and hopefully, we make her laugh. This is because Stormy Daniels is amazing, and let's face it, she has done some pretty brave things over the years. She does stand-up comedy in different parts of the U.S. and has a quick wit. She has been on Saturday's Night Lives and did a really good job.

She does tarot readings for her followers even has a new TV show where she hunts ghosts called Spooky Babes! Our faculty have not seen it yet because our antennae reception in the faculty lounge does not get that channel. Dr. Nelch said he has seen some of Stormy Daniels on film, but we are not sure where he found the films. Maybe he will share some with us in time, and perhaps we could even project them in the small theater on the first floor in the form of a viewing party. Maybe we could invite all the students, the dean, and parents because it is important to pay homage to a celebrity that has your back.

Ms. Stormy is god's gift to the world, and you had better treat her that way, otherwise The Anthropology Department will come after you and send our goons. People can be really mean to her on the Tweeters and we think they are terrible humans. Thank you Ms. Stormy for being extra neat and giving us a bump.

42. Pour Enormous Creativity into Eye-Poppingly Superior T-Shirt Designs

Any anthropologist that is worth their yams knows the best way to advertise how good you are is to make a t-shirt. In fact, our students and faculty are known to design and wear t-shirts on nearly a weekly basis just to commemorate events. What good is it going to an Anthropology Book Club meeting if you do not have a shirt that is date-stamped with that specific day? How will we remember it in perpetuity, or at least until you have to make a donation to Goodwill? Do not fret: if you have to donate some of those shirts they will likely end up on the backs of cultural anthropologists, so you will actually be doing them a favor.

Here at The Anthropology Department, we take enormous pride in the creativity and attention to the visual design of our t-shirts. In fact, many of our shirts take countless hours to design and create. Let us just say that Dr. Chubb really knows what the public likes and how to spice things up visually. In case you are wondering, here are a few examples of our award-winning t-shirts. Feel free to buy them and wear them at a conference because they are super and everyone will like you.

43. Conduct Public Outreach with Local Schools

Listen to this: one of our faculty members once made 19 children at the Collegeville Elementary School cry.

We are proud of this, and you know why? They did not have straight section walls and deserved to be berated by Dr. Nelch for their careless acts of excavation. Let us face it, they were really just digging holes. No attention to the scientific method. No real patience or determination to give us precise replicable data. Just cratering the hell out of that 1960s house foundation like it was a moat they were digging around some insufferable sandcastle at the Indiana Dunes.

Absolutely furious right now as we type this.

How would this situation even come about you might ask? Well, the answer is with public outreach. One of the greatest things an anthropologist can do is show off how neat they are, and what better audience than a classroom full of 2nd graders who will idolize you more than that gold statue on the Indiana James and the Lost Ark movie. This particular incident was especially noteworthy because Dr. Nelch really instilled the fear in those children. The fear of sloppiness. The fear of missing a soil change. The fear of not getting it right. The fear must be taught before you can let go of it.

Many may find our methods a bit non-conventional, or perhaps even overly harsh and draconian. However, it is important to recognize that to get the public on your side, you sometimes need to show those children who is boss. If that means 19 children going home in tears, they learned something for the day that will stick with them their entire lives. They just might turn out to be some of the greatest anthropologists of all time. Right here. Home-grown in Collegeville. Teaching your future field school. You're welcome.

44. Write a Book on How to be the Bestest Anthropologist

They say that those that cannot do, teach. That was clearly written by some half-rate scholar who probably failed at life and whose family likely abandoned them. Here at The Anthropology Department, it is clear that we both *do* and *teach*, which is why you are reading this book right now. We are teaching you the secrets of unlocking your neat self. In the future when you reach your pinnacle, we challenge you to write a self-published book as well. It takes grit, determination, a Jefferson Starship tape, and a lot of Seagram's 7. We look forward to reading your book someday. That way, we can say we were the ones who first planted our anthropological seed in you.

CONCLUSION

You should be literally trembling about anthropology right now.

You are now reincorporated back into society with your fully changed status of powerhouse anthropologist. Do yourself a favor and find a mirror. Gaze upon yourself with admiring eyes. Examine your face. Follow the curves. Ignore the stray eyebrow hair. How has your face changed after reading the advice in this book? If you look closely, you should find it a bit more symmetrical. A bit more youthful. A bit more erudite. Your face should begin to resemble a composite image of all famous anthropologists put together into one.

Now grin at yourself and hold it for 10 seconds. Softly whisper "I anthropology." Repeat this until you feel the strong urge to flip a book table over at a regional conference, or to march over to the Political Science department and tell them they are wrong. Yes. Let that feeling flow through you. We are grinning right now just thinking about you grinning at your grinning reflection. Deep stuff.

You have made it through the most important book that has ever been written about anthropology. This book is a classic, and someone can easily conclude that because we wrote it. The average reader may be a bit confused thinking, "why should I listen to the advice given here?" Well, the answer is because we are smarter than most academics. Not just by a little bit, but by a lot. An average reader might respond with "wow, that's a bold statement, doesn't anthropology teach us that intellect and knowledge are socially constructed?" Yes, they are. And those social constructions still rank us higher. It is just a social fact.

However, because someone has read this book, it means they are one step closer to being as powerhouse as we are. That means a lot. In a sense, their journey will lead them to be the bestest anthropologist they can be, but ultimately, never be better than we are. Which leads us to a concluding point: be humble.

ACKNOWLEDGEMENTS

We acknowledge you, the reader. Also, Jenny and Phil from Texas Roadhouse (they know us, so just say hello whenever you see them).

ABOUT THE AUTHOR

The Chair of The Anthropology Department is the author of numerous self-acclaimed works, including *Being Your Bestest Anthropologist: A Guide To Unlocking Your Neat Self.* The Chair has published over 78 devastating book reviews in prestigious local journals and participated in over 124 regional conferences as both a presenter and attendee. During spare time, The Chair enjoys feeding chipmunks at the Indiana Dunes. The Chair can be reached at anthropologydp@gmail.com for interview requests and celebrity media appearances.

Printed in Great Britain
by Amazon

16332761R00061